Other works by this author:

The Shadow of Kukulkan

Command Screen

Beyond El Camino Del Diablo: Beyond the Devil's Highway

RIO Viejo: Some Memories of Vietnam

(Available only as an e-book from Amazon.com)

ATHIRST
IN
SPIRIT

Eugene Sierras

Order this book online at www.trafford.com
or email orders@trafford.com

Most Trafford titles are also available at major online book retailers.

Print information available on the last page.

ISBN: 978-1-4907-8923-1 (sc)
ISBN: 978-1-4907-8922-4 (hc)
ISBN: 978-1-4907-8924-8 (e)

Library of Congress Control Number: 2018906597

Trafford rev. 06/05/2018

www.trafford.com

North America & international
toll-free: 1 888 232 4444 (USA & Canada)
fax: 812 355 4082

DEDICATION

This is a work of fiction. However, one of the salient premises in the story remains a valid and worthy goal: What was the origin of religion? If we can answer that question, then perhaps we can also determine the origin of man's natural bent for conflict, aggression, and racial hate. If we can, then there may be hope for mitigating that tendency through a greater understanding of its cause or causes with the possibility of finding solutions that may lead to a more peaceful existence among the inhabitants of this planet. Some may find that goal a hopeless folly, but others will realize that it is a worthy ambition and one that merits the challenging search for a viable interdisciplinary synthesis.

When I was an undergraduate student at the University of Arizona majoring in zoology, I read Robert Ardrey's book, *The Territorial Imperative*, written after one of his earlier works, *African Genesis*. I was struck by the scholarship of the author, but even at that stage in my studies, I believed that there was something akin to a spiritual force that was also involved in human evolution. When I read the passage quoted in the epigraph of this work, I found it difficult not to be pessimistic about humankind's future. Perhaps it was my Catholic faith bequeathed to me by my parents, but I sensed, perhaps instinctively, that there was more to human evolution than I had studied. Many years later, I have come to realize that one key difference between the evolution of apes and man is that man has discovered and sought spirituality, including religion.

I believe it is highly likely that his consciousness (introspection) is seeking to communicate with a universal consciousness. I also believe that the impetus for the ancient archetypes in the collective unconscious and origin of religion lies in the ancient events described by Velikovsky and expanded upon by those who have come after.

Over forty years ago, I read Velikovsky's *Worlds in Collision*, and it changed my life's perspective on human history and scientific endeavor. I have eagerly followed the work of those who have expanded and, in some cases, corrected Velikovsky's work. They have labored to provide humanity a new paradigm of cosmology and human history that will present a clearer insight to those who seek answers to determine the ultimate nature of the universe and perhaps human evolution. If we can achieve this greater insight, maybe we can better understand our role within it and with the Almighty.

It is to Velikovsky and to those who have followed and labored to provide us a greater understanding of our universe and our role in it that I dedicate this work.

> *And the Spirit and the bride say, Come. And let him that heareth say, Come. And let him that is* **athirst** *come. And whosoever will, let him take the water of life freely."*

> —Rev. 22:17

> *We were born of risen apes, not fallen angels, and the apes were armed killers besides. And so what shall we wonder at? Our murders and massacres and missiles and irreconcilable regiments? Or our treaties, whatever they may be worth: our symphonies, however seldom they may*

be played; our peaceful acres, however frequently they may be converted into battlefields; our dreams, however rarely they may be accomplished. The miracle of man is not how far he has sunk but how magnificently he has risen.

—Robert Ardrey, *African Genesis*

PREFACE

For thousands of years, religion has had a major impact on human affairs. Prior to the beginning of history, its body of tradition and knowledge were orally transmitted to innumerable generations. It is a large tightly woven thread in the sinuous fiber of the human psyche. Religion is a foundation for millions who recognize and must face mortality. Was there a circumstance on this planet in which religion did not yet exist? Was there even a circumstance on this planet when time as reckoned by humankind did not exist?

Religion has been a force for much good throughout human existence, but it has also been a force for evil. There are times when the boundaries between religion and superstition intersect unevenly and are not precisely recognized. How does one differentiate where that boundary lies?

How does one satisfy the thirst for meaning in life? In Judaism, from which much of Western religious belief and tradition springs, one prominent force was prophecy. Prophecy was a revelation by the divine to a human directly through both dreams and the imaginative faculty (Maimonides words).

The age of prophecy, according to some, has come to an end, although there are still those in modern times who claim to hear the voice of the divine. Maimonides thought that prophecy had come to an end during the Babylonian Exile.[1]

---

[1] Maimonides, *Guide for the Perplexed*, 2:36.

Richard Valencia is in the final years of his life. He has suffered the tragic loss of a young wife and daughter. He has enjoyed a successful marriage of thirty years before the loss to cancer of his second wife. His children have done well in life and remain close to him although separated by distance. He has known the laughter and joy of grandchildren. Yet there remains an empty void in his heart and soul. For several years, he has learned and read about the electric universe, plasma physics, and plasma cosmology based on plasma physics. He has come to understand the consilience of not only scientific disciplines and of the social sciences, including psychology, but also religion and mythology. He has gradually come to the realization that it might be possible to index the progress in interdisciplinary synthesis given impetus by the works of Immanuel Velikovsky. He has enthusiastically engaged himself into writing a book that will encapsulate the progress made in an attempt to determine the origin of religion. He is hopeful that such an index will serve as a datum from which he and others will gain understanding.

Richard has thrown himself into this work for two personal reasons: he believes that an understanding of the origin of religion will provide new insight into his mortality, and he believes this effort to achieve that understanding will mitigate his sorrow and grief over the loss of his wife. He would welcome the religious experience of a prophet touched with the powerful enlightenment by the hand of the divine. Then he would instantly understand that which he seeks. He is resigned, however, to the slow and arduous search, which he is willing to undertake.

ACKNOWLEDGMENTS

I am honored and thankful to Dr. C. Reid Gilbert for reviewing the manuscript and offering insightful comments and recommendations. He is an accomplished author, playwright, poet, college professor, mime, producer, and minister who has published several books.

I am grateful to Barbara Banks for her review of the manuscript and proofreading skills. Her comments and recommendations greatly assisted me.

I would like to thank Honey Mason for her close scrutiny and correction of my many grammar transgressions. She is a retired schoolteacher whose experience in grading papers was extremely beneficial to the final product.

Any faults or errors that succeed in remaining undetected are solely my fault and only mine.

PROLOGUE

"Come, Dad, it is time to go. Everyone else has left, and I'm cold," Sarah said. She looked at her husband, Andrew. "Don't you agree?"

"Sarah's right, Dad," Andrew said. "It's not only that she's pregnant, but the temperature is also rapidly dropping, and the rain is turning to sleet."

Richard Valencia turned to his daughter. "You're right, Sarah. I'm sorry. It's difficult to leave your mother here, but it's time to go." He turned to his son, Michael, who stood solemnly at his mother's grave, standing as if at attention in the dress blues of a second lieutenant in the United States Army. "Come, Michael, Sarah's right. The weather is bitter, and we can remember her in the warmth of our family at home."

The four of them walked to the car and entered. Andrew was in the driver's seat with Sarah at his side. Richard turned to look one last time at Rachel's grave. He softly whispered goodbye and then sat in the back seat and closed the door.

"Who would have thought," Richard said, "that the weather would be so bad here in Tucson when I buried my wife?"

"Dad," Sarah said, "you know she's in a better place now where her pain and suffering are over. We did everything possible to fight her cancer, but it was her time to be called by God."

"Called by God to where?" Michael asked his sister. "To Sheol[2]? Dad, I like your Catholic's version of paradise better. I prefer to believe that Mom is in a happy and peaceful place."

Richard smiled at his son seated next to him. He took his hand in his and tried to comfort him in his grief for his mother.

"Michael, I converted to Judaism from my Catholic faith because of your mother. She taught us that Judaism believes that heaven is not a community exclusive to the people of only one faith but is inclusive for the righteous of any people. In fact, she taught me that the belief in an afterlife is as diverse as Judaism itself and includes everything from the reunification of the flesh and the body when the Messiah comes to a spiritual existence."

"I'm sorry that Mother won't get to hold her first grandchild, but I know that she will be nearby," Sarah said, placing her hand on her abdomen.

"When will we know whether it's a boy or a girl?" Michael asked.

"Normally after sixteen weeks, Michael. I'm scheduled for a sonogram in three weeks. I'll let you and Dad know as soon as I do."

Later, the family sat in the family room next to a hearty fire and sipped hot chocolate and hot apple cider with cinnamon. They spoke fondly of their memories of Rachel Valencia, wife and mother.

"What will you do now, Dad?" Sarah asked.

"I'll be OK, Sarah. You don't have to worry about me. I've been volunteering for a couple of organizations. One provides delivery of hot meals to those who are essentially homebound. I also sometimes volunteer at the Veterans Administration Hospital when they have special events. Recently, I've read reviews of a book that seems interesting and which I intend to get soon and read."

---

[2] Eccles. 9:6. Sheol, the place in the afterlife where the dead go.

Two days later, Richard sat alone next to the fire. His children had both called to let him know they had safely returned to their homes. Sarah and Andrew were back in Colorado, and Michael was back at Fort Benning, Georgia, to begin his ranger training. He looked at the book sitting on the table next to the recliner in which he sat, which was *Worlds in Collision*[3] by Immanuel Velikovsky. He had completed it in two lengthy sessions, not being able to easily set it down. He intended to read it again more studiously and take notes. His research on the Internet had led him to additional sources about some of the ideas in the book. Two that he intended to do further reading about were the electric universe and plasma physics.

Richard had long wondered about religion and what lay beyond death. With the recent loss of Rachel, he became determined to seek out as much knowledge as possible and to write it down so he could more easily understand what he learned. Little did he realize that his effort would develop into a lengthy research effort and would culminate in writing a book. He instinctively knew that his determination would not only serve to focus his life in a meaningful effort but would also hopefully provide a greater understanding of life and death and would perhaps serve to mitigate his grief and sorrow.

---

[3] Immanuel Velikovsky, *Worlds in Collision* (Garden City, New York: Doubleday & Company, Inc., 1950).

CONTENTS

CHAPTER ONE

NAOMI SVERDLOV

Richard entered Interstate 10 from the Benson Highway and accelerated. The woman announcer was giving the most recent update of Tucson traffic on the radio. She said that Speedway at Stone was completely blocked by a three-vehicle collision. He decided to change his route from Speedway. He would exit at Congress Street to take Broadway Boulevard to the university. He glanced at the dashboard clock. It was twenty minutes until his ten-o-clock appointment with Professor Glickman. He would make it on time he thought as he exited the interstate on the off-ramp to Congress Street.

He had just said goodbye to his daughter, Sarah, and three grandchildren—Nathan, Skyler, and Olivia—who were returning to their home in Denver. Sarah had made it a point to visit him frequently. She wanted to ensure that he was not drifting off into loneliness and grief since the passing of his wife and her mother, Rachel. He smiled at the thought of his daughter being so concerned. It had been over six years since Rachel had passed from breast cancer, and Sarah was still worried.

Richard braked as traffic slowed considerably a block west of the United States Federal Courthouse. He looked ahead at what was a large gathering of people carrying signs and several police cars with their red-and-blue lights flashing. He rolled down the SUV's windows to better hear his surroundings. He briefly came to a stop and addressed a police officer standing on the sidewalk, wearing a bright yellow traffic vest.

"Excuse me, Officer, what's going on?" he asked.

"There's a protest demonstration ahead at the federal courthouse, sir. Traffic is slow, but it will be unimpeded," he replied.

"What's the occasion?" he asked.

"There is a couple of Border Patrol buses bringing several illegal aliens to their court hearing, and people are protesting that they're not getting a fair trial. So far, it's been peaceful."

"Thanks, Officer," Richard said as he again started moving forward.

He arrived ahead of the cars behind him as the traffic light changed to red at Granada Avenue and Congress Street in front of the courthouse. Standing on the corner was a man who held a Mexican flag in one hand and a long butane lighter in the other. Richard used a similar one himself to light his grill for backyard barbecues.

"Are you going to set that flag on fire?" Richard called out to him.

The man turned his eyes and looked at him for several seconds before he spoke. In those several seconds, a strong emotion surged through Richard. The subject to whom he addressed his question was a man in his late forties or early fifties with a salt-and-pepper beard and mustache. Both were neatly trimmed. He wore a ball cap with an insignia on it that Richard could not make out. He was about six feet two inches or so and probably about two hundred to two hundred twenty pounds. Although he had a middle-aged belly, he was in good shape and obviously strong from the appearance of his burly arms, chest, and shoulders. He wore an open brown leather vest over a T-shirt and blue denims. On his feet were dusty ankle-high leather work boots.

He gazed at Richard with a questioning look, which seemed to indicate he was undecided whether Richard would be an ally or a foe.

"Why?" Richard asked him.

"I'm sick and tired of these damn Mexicans invading our country, taking away our jobs, and sponging off our welfare. They need to go back to Mexico where they came from. They don't belong here."

Richard recognized the hatred that now glared at him through the man's steel blue eyes.

The man turned his attention to the flag in his hands, and with a couple of strikes with the lighter's trigger, a bright blue flame appeared, which he held to the flag. In seconds, the flag began to burn.

"Put that fire out immediately!" a voice commanded.

Richard turned to see two police officers in full riot gear approach the man, who stood defiantly, awaiting them. He also became aware of a young woman reporter holding a microphone, followed by a photographer with a large camera mounted on his shoulder at some distance behind the man. Several protesters began to leave the curb across the street from the courthouse where police barricades manned by officers had kept them.

"Get moving, sir," a third officer also in full riot gear ordered him, although the light was still red. "Move it!"

Richard complied, slowly driving through the intersection, which was rapidly becoming filled with what appeared to be both protesters and counterprotesters. Many were holding signs and American and Mexican flags. There was a disciplined line of police, again in full riot gear, which was also slowly moving into the intersection in a coordinated movement to control the crowd.

Once he had driven beyond the intersection, the street was free of pedestrians, and most of the traffic had moved ahead of him while he was stopped at the light. He thought of the emotion that had surged through him when he saw the man with the flag. Richard was not sure if his brief encounter was with a white supremacist or just a disgruntled man afraid of change, but he had experienced similar adrenaline-charged emotion when he had killed an avowed white supremacist at his wife's office almost thirty years ago.

Get ahold of yourself, Richard. Pursed-lip breathe. Concentrate on getting to your appointment safely.

He thought of Rachel, whom he had been with when she was attacked by two white supremacists all those years ago. He had reacted as he had trained and prepared himself, to respond to an immediate threat to her. He had killed her attacker and never regretted it. He had also lost a dear friend, a young woman employee whom he and Rachel had hired to serve as her bodyguard. Before she was killed, she had fatally wounded a second attacker, but the loss and grief from her violent death were life lasting. He resolved to put the memory and emotional response into the compartment of his mind, which he had learned to temporarily send memories and thoughts to until he was in a better circumstance to think about them. It was a skill he had learned while flying into combat during his naval service.

He arrived at the university campus a few minutes before ten. He hurriedly parked in the Sixth Street Garage, entering on Lowell Street, and made his way to the social science building on South Campus Drive. He arrived at the Judaic Studies office five minutes after ten o'clock.

"Have a seat, Mr. Valencia. Dr. Glickman just phoned that he will be a few minutes late. He was returning from the airport and was delayed in traffic downtown because of some sort of protest," Jane Ryder, the receptionist, advised him.

"I understand," Richard replied. "I also got caught in traffic near the U.S. Courthouse returning from the airport. There was a protest demonstration there."

"That's where Professor Glickman is coming from. He was there to pick up Dr. Naomi Sverdlov, who will be a guest lecturer in the beginning Hebrew course you'll be taking."

"I'm impressed. Isn't it unusual for a visiting doctor to assist in teaching a beginning Hebrew course?"

"Dr. Glickman loves to teach this continuing education course because many of his students like you are professionals in other occupations who are taking this course for cultural enrichment as well as learning Hebrew. Dr. Sverdlov, whom the professor knows well from his travels to Israel, is a paleographer who specializes in ancient writings. Dr. Glickman believes she will add quite a perspective on studying the development of the Hebrew alphabet that will enrich the course. However, the primary purpose of her visit is to participate in a roundtable discussion at the College of Anthropology. The college will be sponsoring and conducting an advanced honors course on the Dead Sea Scrolls during the summer of 2015 in Jerusalem. Participants at the roundtable discussion will be from several departments, including the Department of Religious Studies in the College of Humanities."

"I certainly look forward to meeting Dr. Sverdlov," Richard replied.

"Excuse me," Jane said as she answered the telephone.

He sat in his chair in the lobby of the Judaic Studies office, waiting for his language instructor to arrive and to think about the course he had eagerly enrolled in. He had learned Hebrew from a previous undergraduate course he had taken after his conversion to Judaism at the Reform University Synagogue. Both he and his wife, Rachel, were members. She had greatly assisted him by speaking only Hebrew on certain evenings of the week. After the children arrived, they continued the practice of having Hebrew-only evenings and also, at her insistence, Spanish-only evenings. Rachel had become fluent in Spanish because she felt it necessary to better represent her clients as an immigration attorney. Many of her clients could not speak English or only spoke and understood a limited amount. As a result of their efforts and enrolling the children in schools that taught both Hebrew and Spanish, their daughter and son had grown up fluent in three languages. The children had also picked up a conversational familiarity with Yiddish from visiting Rachel's parents and relatives. Richard himself, who had similarly experienced Spanish-only evenings with his sister when he was a child, had become significantly more proficient in the language after he had met Rachel.

His mind began to return to the episode he had experienced earlier with his thoughts about Rachel. Before he could begin, Dr. Glickman and a woman walked through the door.

"I see you made it!" Jane greeted them with a smile. "You must be Dr. Sverdlov." She smiled as she stood and extended her hand to the woman.

While the trio exchanged greetings, Richard studied the woman. She was about fifty to fifty-five years old, he surmised. She had dark hair streaked with strands of gray, which she wore short and which complemented her attractive face. Her dark eyes glanced toward him as she observed him and smiled. She was about five feet four inches or so, the same height as Rachel. She was dressed in a dark pin-striped skirt and jacket over a white blouse. She wore stockings visible under her skirt, which fell below her knees. He noticed she wore what he considered comfortable low-heel black shoes.

Dr. Glickman noticed her glance toward Richard and greeted him, "Hello, Richard. Sorry we're late. We had a bit of a delay passing the federal courthouse downtown. I thought we would avoid Speedway because of an accident at Stone. It goes to illustrate that not all shortcuts are successful."

"I also was slightly delayed by the same route. I was returning from the airport after seeing my daughter and grandchildren off."

"Let me introduce the two of you," Dr. Glickman said.

Richard stood and extended his hand toward the woman as the doctor spoke. "Naomi, this is Richard Valencia, who, together with his late wife, was and is a member of our Reform University Synagogue. Richard, this is Dr. Naomi Sverdlov, a highly respected and esteemed paleographer, who lives and works in Israel."

"It is a pleasure to meet you, Richard. Will you be a student in Dr. Glickman's Hebrew class?"

"It is my pleasure to meet you, Naomi. I hope your stay in Tucson will be pleasant. Yes, I will be in Dr. Glickman's class. I understand from speaking with Jane that you will be making a presentation as well," Richard replied in his best Hebrew.

"My, what a surprise," Naomi said. "You speak good Hebrew although with a noticeable American accent. Why, may I ask, are you taking a beginning Hebrew class?"

Richard smiled. "I must compliment you on your English. You have only a slight Israeli accent. If I hadn't spent as much time in Israel as I have, I probably would not have noticed it. I'm taking Dr. Glickman's course because I desire to improve my Hebrew comprehension. An advanced Hebrew course right now would be too difficult for me."

"Richard is working on a book that includes ancient Hebrew references. I haven't mentioned you to him until now that you will be making a presentation during the course on Hebrew paleography. I'm sure he will be greatly interested.

"Listen, why don't the two of you come into my office and we will complete Richard's registration? Then we can ensure Naomi's quarters and living arrangements are all set. I was planning to take Naomi to the faculty dining room in the student union for lunch before she checks in at her hotel. Richard, we would love to have you join us for lunch at noon if you're available."

"Yes. Thank you, Doctor. I'll be there."

"Also, Richard, both Naomi and I discussed the fact that we prefer to be on a first-name basis. Sometimes in the company of so many people who have the degree, it gets confusing and a little awkward."

"Yes, Peter. I'll try to remember that."

After Richard left the office, he walked directly to the university bookstore, where he spent over an hour perusing the numerous books available. He glanced at the clock on the university bookstore wall. It was eleven forty-five, and he needed to start toward the faculty dining facility here in the student union. He had found one of Naomi Sverdlov's books in the Judaic Studies section titled *A Guide to the Script of the Dead Sea Scrolls*. He had learned from the flyleaf that Naomi Sverdlov was a professor of paleography and epigraphy at the Jerusalem University, where she currently lived. She had immigrated to Israel from Russia several years ago as did her late husband, although they didn't meet until after they had lived in Israel. She had published several scholarly books and other works. He quickly paid for the book and walked to the dining room. When he entered the room, he saw Peter Glickman and Naomi seated with two men and a woman at a table. As he approached the table, the men stood, and Peter introduced him to Arnold Wiseman and Keith Oliver, who were professors at the College of Anthropology. The woman was Peter's wife, Francine.

During the meal, the conversation turned to the roundtable discussion. Professor Wiseman mentioned that Jane Barker would also make a presentation at the round table.

"Jane Barker?" Naomi asked. "Dr. Jane Elizabeth Barker, professor of religion at Harvard University?"

"She's actually retired now, Naomi," Arnold Wiseman replied. "She is in Tucson, living with her daughter, who is caring for her while she recovers from chemotherapy treatment for uterine cancer. She is doing quite well, I understand, from my recent conversation with her daughter, Rebecca Stover. I learned of her being here in Tucson quite by accident. A good friend of mine happened to see her and her daughter shopping downtown several weeks ago and mentioned it to me. I was able to track down her daughter's phone number and called her. After introducing myself, I asked if I could speak to her mother. When Jane came to the phone, she was delighted to speak with me. I mentioned to her the university's honors course in Jerusalem this summer and the roundtable discussion. When I asked her if she would speak at the discussion, she readily agreed. I have since met her twice. She appears to be in good health and tells me that her cancer is in remission. Do you know her, Naomi?"

"Yes. She is world renowned! She has published several scholarly works on religious history, mostly the Christian faith, and has appeared on several World History Channel programs as an expert in her field, which she most certainly is. She has also appeared on several programs produced and presented by the Public Television Channel here in the United States. I have had the pleasure of meeting her on two occasions, both during filming of programs on which we both appeared. I'm so glad she's here. I am looking forward to meeting her again and talking with her.

"We do have some things in common beyond our interest and work in religion. She lost her husband several years ago to a stroke as did I with my husband, Yacov. I have read many of her works, but I believe one of her most profound is one in which she discusses the Gospel of Thomas, one of the Nag Hammadi manuscripts. Like me and many other scholars who have studied that manuscript, there is no doubt that the Gnostics believed that Christ was a man who was sent to teach us that the kingdom of heaven is within us. That is not inconsistent with my interpretation of Jewish belief. In fact, the early Christian Gnostics were almost all Jewish."

"Well, you most certainly will meet her," Arnold said, "since you both will be honored speakers at our roundtable discussion."

Lunch was a pleasant affair. At the end, everyone stood and expressed their pleasure at meeting new people and that they all looked forward to meeting again.

Richard said goodbye to Naomi and asked, "Naomi, would you be kind and autograph this work of yours for me? I can't wait to read it."

"Of course, I will! Thank you for your purchase. Peter told me briefly about your work in progress. Apparently, you gave him a copy of one of your preliminary drafts. It is most interesting to me since I believe one of the theses you write about is the common origin of religion. He also told me a little about your wife and your loss. I hope we can meet again perhaps over lunch and continue to learn more about each other and especially what I consider to be your interesting thesis."

"I also would love to do that. Let me get in touch with you through Peter, and we can arrange a lunch date during what I am certain is your very busy schedule. I also must tell you that I am somewhat humbled by the advanced degrees you and others possess. I have only my bachelor of science degree. Furthermore, I am not a Talmudic scholar. I hope you don't think it presumptuous of me to participate in your scholarly discussions."

"Absolutely not. Some of the best advances in any discipline have come from those who labor with a passion outside the scope of a mainstream discipline. What was your degree in?"

"It's in aeronautical engineering from Old Dominion University in Norfolk, Virginia. I've also later received a second bachelor in electrical engineering while I was on active duty with the navy."

"Very briefly, Richard, how does your engineering background bring you to an interest in Hebrew?"

"I need to be proficient enough in Hebrew to read some of the source documents of religious texts I need to understand for my book."

"I am fascinated by your thesis. Dr. Glickman very briefly summarized it for me. Do you think we could get together one evening for a discussion about your work without having to worry about after lunch engagements? I am fascinated by it."

"Of course. I assume you'll be busy the next day or so with arrangements for your presentation in Hebrew class and at the round table. I'll call you soon, and maybe we can have dinner, and I can answer any questions you may have."

"I would love that. You can reach me through Dr. Glickman. I look forward to speaking further with you. Shalom, Richard.

"Shalom, Naomi."

CHAPTER TWO

SHURA VEGA

Capt. Michael Valencia walked out of the field headquarters of the PUK's first brigade and looked toward the west. He saw a group of five individuals approaching the headquarters, but they were still far enough away that he could not determine which one was Shura. He had not seen her for almost five days. Her company had been involved in heavy combat with ISIS forces several kilometers southwest of the headquarters, which was some fifteen kilometers southwest of Bardarash in Kirkuk province.

He again quietly whispered the part of the Israeli prayer that Shura had taught him, "May it be your will, Adonai our God, that they be guided safely and protected against every enemy and harm. May their path be successful and guard their going out and coming in to life and peace now and forever."[4]

He had unexpectedly met Shura two weeks after he had reported for duty as an American Army advisor to the first brigade of Peshmerga's PUK. The PUK, or Patriotic Union of Kurdistan, was one of the military forces fighting for the autonomous government of Iraq's Kurdistan. Unlike American forces, which were under a unified command structure, the military forces of Iraqi Kurdistan are divided and controlled

---

[4] Adapted from the Israel Movement for Progressive Judaism's siddur (prayer book), *http://www.reformjudaism.org/practice/prayers-blessings/ may-one-who-blessed-our-fighters.*

12

separately by the PUK and the KDP or the Democratic Party of Kurdistan. The KDP allows women in their ranks but only as support troops and not on the front lines unlike the PUK, which has several hundred women in frontline combat units. That was why Shura and her friends had volunteered to fight for the PUK. He knew she and her two friends had gone to Israel and enlisted in the Israeli Defense Forces (IDF) but never expected to see her or them again in Iraq.

Michael had fallen in love with the independent and attractive woman soldier, and he truly believed she loved him as well. How would she take the news of his impending departure? She had also told him that she believed it was time for her to return to Israel and thence to her native Mexico. He hoped he could convince her to stop in Tucson so he could take her to his father again. They had met when they both attended the University of Arizona and had occasionally dated when they were students until their senior year when they began to steadily date. She had previously met his parents before his mother's passing in 2007. Shura had been deeply affected by her studies of the Holocaust while at the university, and it was for that reason that she had immigrated to Israel with two friends to join the Israeli Defense Forces. All three had enlisted in the Israeli army. One of her friends, a local Tucson girl, Elisha Lipowitz, had made Aliya[5] with her and a male friend from her community in Mexico City. Elisha had been killed in action while in Iraq. The other friend, Shlomo Horowitz, had also made Aliya to Israel with her and Elisha after graduating from the University of Arizona. He had chosen to return to Israel after one year's service with the PUK.

Shura had experienced combat in the IDF and attained the rank of sergeant. When her enlistment was up, she decided to travel to northern Iraq with her two friends to join forces with the Peshmerga, again deeply affected by the cruel treatment of people by the Islamic State in Syria and Iraq (ISIS).

---

[5] Immigration of Jews to Eretz Israel (land of Israel).

He smiled when the group had approached close enough for him to recognize her in full battle gear. She smiled at him as she approached, and they hugged. He wanted to kiss her. The rules for patronization between officers and enlisted were not as strict as in the American Army. The Peshmerga were a highly disciplined and trained fighting force, and he did not want to violate tradition or regulations of the soldiers he had come to admire and respect.

"Shura, thank God, you are well. How was the firefight?"

"Hello, Michael. I am very happy to see that you are also in good health. It was intensive. We were attacked by several ISIS suicide bombers, some with explosives in their vehicles that sped toward us. We were successful in destroying the vehicles before they could inflict damage on us. Thank God, we had only minor casualties."

They looked into each other's eyes, and he knew that she loved him.

"I have news to tell you," he said. "I've received my orders for rotation back to the States. I've been given thirty days' leave en route. I hope to see my father in Tucson. Shura, you've told me that you believed the time was approaching for you also to return to Israel and then Mexico to visit your family. I want and hope that we can arrange to spend time together in Tucson. I want very much to reintroduce you to my father."

"When will you be leaving?"

"In two weeks. I will report to my headquarters in Bagdad for debriefing then on to the States, where I have to report to Special Operations Command at Fort Bragg. After in-processing, I'll take leave. I want very much to meet you in Tucson. What do you think?"

"I would love to! Are you sure, Michael? In my family, when a girl brings a boy home to meet her family, it is because they are serious about each other. I'm a woman, not a girl, and you're a man, not a boy, but I want to know how you feel about me."

"Shura, I love you. I want to marry you and spend the rest of my life with you."

"I love you as well, Michael. Is this a proposal?"

"I can't get down on my knee to ask you here, Shura, not in front of our comrades. I don't have a ring. I promise I'll ask you properly in Tucson."

"Michael, I also want to spend the rest of my life with you. I want us to have a family. I'm leaving the military for a normal life. Will you stay in the army?"

"No. I'm thinking of getting out of the army altogether. I've discussed my intentions with Major Kensington, my commanding officer. He told me I was up for promotion to major and that if I decided to join the reserves, I would do so in that rank."

"Are you seriously considering the reserves? You would probably still be away for a great deal of time for training and actual deployment."

"No. It's time for us to start a new life together, Shura. I too want to start a family. I might have to go back to school for a master's in business. I'm not sure I can make a living and support a family with only my army experience in the civilian world."

"There is always Israel. I remember you telling me you spent time there with your family as a child. You speak passable Hebrew. That's always an option."

"We'll have plenty of time to talk about our future together. What I want most of all is to place a ring on your finger and marry you."

"As do I," she replied and quickly kissed him on the lips. "I don't care who sees us now."

CHAPTER THREE

JANE BARKER

Richard was returning from the mailbox, looking through the letters and magazines he had retrieved, when he heard the telephone ring. He quickly glanced at one envelope, which he recognized was sent from Michael. He smiled with joy at receiving the letter from his son as he hurried up the steps and through the front door to answer the telephone.

"Hello, this is Richard," he greeted.

"Richard, this is Naomi. How are you?"

"Hello, Naomi. What a pleasant surprise! I'm fine, thank you. How are you? I hope your visit in Tucson is going well."

"It's been a real pleasure, Richard. Peter and Francine have been wonderful hosts, and I find associating with Peter's colleagues extremely interesting. They are dedicated to making the university's honors course in Jerusalem as successful as possible, and they are expending a tremendous amount of effort in planning for it.

"The reason I called is that I recently learned that I will be free tomorrow night. I am taking you up on your offer for dinner and discussion about your current work. Are you available?"

"Yes, I am, and I'm looking forward to it. Tell me, is there a favorite cuisine or restaurant that you may have heard about here in Tucson?"

"Actually, there is. I've had an opportunity to sample some local Mexican food, and I love it! If you know a good Mexican restaurant, I would love to eat there."

"I do. There is a family restaurant that has been a mainstay of the locals in Barrio Magdalena just south of downtown. The food is superb, although the atmosphere is more folksy than elegant."

"I would love to go there! I myself am much more 'folksy' than elegant. I do have a favor to ask you."

"Please, Naomi, tell me."

"I've been fortunate to meet Jane Barker and have been able to speak with her briefly during our meetings with the roundtable planning group. I mentioned you and your work and the fact we agreed to get together for a leisurely dinner one evening to have a discussion uninterrupted by any demands for our time. She told me she would love to meet you and said she thought it would be interesting to hear what you had to say about your project. It would also give us all an opportunity to get to know one another better and discuss whatever we desire to. She said she has also grown fond of Mexican food while living with her daughter here."

"Good. I'll make reservations for three tomorrow evening at seven. I can pick you up at your hotel at six o'clock, and then we can pick up Jane at her daughter's house after that. Do you have her address?"

"No, not yet, but I told her I would call her as soon as our plans were firmed and I'll get her daughter's address then. I'm staying in room 226 at the university hotel. I'm sure you know where it is. I'll be waiting for you in the lobby."

"I'm looking forward to seeing you again and meeting Jane. I'll see you tomorrow at six."

"Thank you, Richard. Shalom."

"Shalom."

Richard smiled as he placed the telephone on its cradle. He liked Naomi and found her fascinating. He had read her book that he had purchased at the university bookstore and found it extremely professionally written as well as engrossing. He realized the great amount of study and labor it took to be able to understand and interpret what to many would appear to be unintelligible markings on a medium of papyrus, stone, or clay. He had also read a little about Jane Barker. He intended to learn more about this remarkable woman. He would have to do it quickly before tomorrow evening.

He grabbed a pitcher of tea from the refrigerator and filled a tall tumbler with it before taking it and Michael's letter to the recliner in the living room. He opened the envelope and read the letter.

> *January 15, 2015*
> *Combined Joint Task Force*
> *Operation Inherent Resolve*
> *Bagdad, Republic of Iraq (Al Jumhuriyah al Iraqiyah)*
>
> *Dear Dad,*
> *I hope this letter finds you well. It's been almost a year since my assignment to the CTF's Operation Inherent Resolve, and I am due to rotate home. By the time you receive this letter, I will be well on my way from Bagdad to Fort Bragg, North Carolina. After in-processing at my new command, I will be on thirty days' leave and plan on coming to Tucson and spend some time with you. I hope my old room is still available!*
> *I will be seeing Shura Vega. I think you remember her. She was a student at the University of Arizona when I was there, and we became friends. We dated on and off our first two years and pretty steady during our last year. I brought her to dinner one evening, and you and Mom both met her, and from what I can remember, you both liked her very much. Although she is Orthodox, she attended several Shabbat services with us at the*

university synagogue. She became fond of the Mishkan T'filah,[6] although she grew up with the orthodox siddur in Mexico City. I remember that Mom liked her. She was saddened when Mom passed.

Dad, she is a remarkable woman! I'll refresh your memory in case you're getting to that age where things get a little difficult to recall (just kidding). She was born and raised in Mexico City to Orthodox parents. She received a typical education like others in her peer group until high school when her circle of friends began to expand. She had a strong crush on a boy her age that wasn't Jewish but was from a prominent family. The boy's name was Jorge Gastelum, as I remember, and his father, Mauricio, was a prominent employee of the Mexican Finance Ministry or Secretaría de Hacienda y Crédito Público. He introduced her to a new circle of friends outside the closely knit Jewish community. Her parents began to worry when they thought the two of them were getting serious, but to hear Shura tell about it, she was fascinated with the world outside the narrow circle she had been brought up in. I remember her telling me that intermarriage between Mexico City Jews and Gentiles was almost unheard of. I don't think they are as closed as the Hasidim, but they definitely mostly live within their community.

I've come to know Shura a lot better now than when we were in school. She is a seasoned combat soldier who served three years in the Israeli Defense Forces, where she attained the rank of sergeant in the infantry. She was deeply moved by the reports of extreme cruelty that began to come out of Iraq when ISIS came to power and conquered large swaths of Iraq, especially in those regions that contained religious minority elements. One of the reasons for her moving to Israel and becoming a citizen with dual status with Mexico is because she

---

[6] Reform Judaism siddur or prayer book, *http://www.jewishbookcouncil.org/book/mishkan-tfilah.*

was deeply affected by her studies of the Holocaust. She took the extremely surprising step (to others as well as me) when she left Israel to volunteer with the Peshmerga in Iraqi Kurdistan. When she learned that the PUK or the Patriotic Union of Kurdistan was the only part of the Peshmerga that allowed women into combat units, she signed up with them. She told me recently when we declared our love for each other that she was leaving Iraq for Israel and would return to her home in Mexico City. We agreed to meet in Tucson, where I would properly propose to her.

Dad, I have fallen in love with her and, as I mentioned, kind of informally proposed to her in Iraq with a promise to do so properly when we are in Tucson. It seems counterintuitive to tell you how sensitive and caring she is. She is deeply religious but in a more spiritual than ritualistic way. She is definitely the woman I want to spend my life and start a family with! We will both be leaving the military for civilian life. I'll tell you more about our plans in person.

Don't write me at this address because I will probably be arriving back in the States by the time you receive it, and I will call as soon as I can. Tell Sarah and Drew that I hope to see them soon. Hopefully, Sarah will remember Shura.

Be well, Dad. I look forward to seeing you soon.

Love,
Michael

Richard put down the letter and smiled at the words his son had written. Michael was now twenty-eight years old, two years older than he when he married his mother, Rachel, and four years older than when he had married his first wife, Catherine. Richard didn't worry about his son's love life, but he knew it was good that his son had found a woman he loved and with whom he wanted to share his life. Although Michael had graduated with a business degree with a major in finance, his experience with Army ROTC at the university convinced him he wanted to serve in the army and perhaps even make it a career. From what he knew about his son's experience, Michael had proven himself to be a capable soldier and officer and an excellent leader. He had a good résumé for future promotion and assignment.

He didn't blame his son for wanting to return to civilian life and start a family. Richard had been on active duty with the navy when he met Catherine, his first wife. He had been fortunate that he had experienced a deep love for her, a love that she had reciprocated. Together, they had a beautiful daughter, Bernadette. Although he had long accepted their untimely death, a feeling of sadness overcame him as he recalled the skipper of his fighter squadron and the ship's chaplain informing him of the event that took their lives on the same day. Catherine had suffered a ruptured brain aneurysm and collapsed in the kitchen while waiting for a neighbor to visit with her daughter, also two years old, for a playdate with Bernadette. After witnessing her mother's collapse, his daughter had become distraught and wandered into the backyard. The gate to the pool was closed but not latched, and Bernadette had opened it and wandered into the pool area, where she apparently fell in and drowned. By the time the neighbor lady arrived with her daughter and called 911, it was too late to revive his daughter. His wife was rushed to the emergency room at the hospital, where she died.

He didn't linger on his memories of his flight off the USS *Eisenhower* in the Persian Gulf or the activities leading to his wife and daughter's burial in the family plot in Virginia Beach next to his father's grave. He recalled that he had sold his house and possessions and had driven cross-country in a new truck to Yuma, where he intended to travel El Camino del Diablo, the Devil's Highway. He and his father had long talked and planned one day to make the trek in memory of Richard's great-great-grandfather, Francisco, who had done so as a fourteen-year-old forty-niner in 1849. It was after that trip and meeting people who were involved with Rachel that he had met her. He was still grieving over Catherine and Bernadette and not seeking another woman when she came into his life. They fell in love and married. He was fortunate to have met her and for the two beautiful children they shared. Rachel was a woman of deep faith, who was able to accept the knowledge of her impending death with grace and placed her trust in Hashem. It was because of Rachel that Richard had converted to Judaism. He had been raised as Roman Catholic but had never been one to be pious or observant. Both of them were comfortable and happy in their shared faith. Both their children reflected her deep faith and goodwill toward others. That was her legacy.

Richard chuckled when recalled the words Michael had written that he hoped his old room was still available. Two years after Rachel's passing, he sold the family home and bought a smaller townhouse away from the central part of the city. His townhouse was on an acre of land and included a two-bedroom guesthouse. Richard hoped that his children and grandchildren would visit him often enough that the guesthouse would be well used.

Richard placed the letter on the small table in the den as he walked in and sat at his computer. He typed in the words "Jane Barker and Harvard University." With an amazing speed that never ceased to amaze him, a list of several pages of information about Jane Barker and Harvard University appeared on the screen. After twenty minutes of intensive reading, he took a break to refill his glass with ice tea and then sat at the computer to digest the information about Jane Barker in front of him.

Before her retirement because of health reasons, she had held the Victor R. Bellow chair of religion at the Divinity School. Before that, she held several professorships at various universities, including Princeton and Cornell. She had published several books on religion and religious history, including the Gnostic gospels, the divinity of Christ, and Mary Magdalene.

She was born in Washington State in 1952 and attended local schools through high school. She received a scholarship to the University of California at Berkeley, where she received her

MA in religious history. According to her biography, she had originally intended to major in dance. She continued on with her graduate work at Harvard, where she completed her PhD in religious history, having written her thesis on the Nag Hammadi manuscripts.

She had married in her late twenties and had a daughter whom she now lived with here in Tucson. She had lost her husband seven years ago to a stroke. He looked at her photograph on the Harvard website. He reckoned she must have been in her late forties or early fifties when the portrait was taken. It was an attractive woman who gazed at him from the computer screen.

He looked forward to dinner with both women, whom he each considered extremely interesting and accomplished in their respective fields. Naomi had assured him that his lack of an advanced degree was not a great concern of hers. He wondered how Jane would feel about having dinner with an engineer. Naomi had said that she was interested in his work. The main thesis in his work was the origin of religion. Obviously, a woman with her and Jane's background would probably be interested in such a topic. *I wonder if they'll be disappointed,* he thought.

Richard was writing the book not as an original researcher but to express his interpretation of the rigorous interdisciplinary work that had been accomplished in the field of plasma physics and the electric universe.[7] He had originally begun his work as a personal effort to comprehend the world about him and to try to answer some basic questions of the nature and structure of the world, including the universe, life, and religion. The more he read and studied, the more he began to realize that all things were truly connected. His original entrée into his work was religion. Raised by moderately devout Catholic parents, he had converted to Reform Judaism when he had met and married Rachel. He had suffered the loss of two women he loved and a beautiful daughter, but he had never known the bitterness

---

[7] The Electric Universe Theory Wiki *http://www.electricuniverse.info/Introduction*

and resentment of others he knew who had suffered tragic loss in their lives. He had been fortunate and was grateful to have known the love of two beautiful and wonderful women and three beautiful children, not to mention his grandchildren. Still, as he approached the autumn of his years, he sought more knowledge about his origin, the meaning of his life, and his ultimate destiny. Religion was a strong force in human affairs and history. Both he and his son had fought Islamic extremists, but he was well aware that religious extremism was not restricted to those of the Muslim faith.

Richard was adamant that he thoroughly research and document the work of others to avoid what he considered a potential pitfall. He did not want to begin his exploration into the origin of religion based on false assumptions. Some of the greatest thinkers of the twentieth century published brilliant and detailed theses based on erroneous assumptions. Einstein's brilliant work on general relativity dealt with the laws of gravity, which, he assumed, governed the movements of large bodies. However, although the assumption that gravity was the primary force and mover in the universe was prevalent during the period of his work, gravity is not the primary force of the universe. Stephen Hawking, another brilliant mind, spent considerable time attempting to find the grand unified theory, which would resolve the contradictions between relativity and quantum mechanics. It is highly likely that gravity is one aspect of the electromagnetic force.

He sat back in his chair and reflected on the upcoming dinner with two very interesting women. He had spent the early years after Rachel had died working as a consultant for a contractor who was working with the U.S. Navy on a new weapon system for the Super Hornet FA-18/F. That work had slowed after the successful completion of that project and as he had aged and had not been able to keep up with the new advances in navy weaponry, much of which was classified in the development stages. It had been interesting work, but when that opportunity diminished, he had sought volunteer work. He had served with an organization that delivered meals to elderly and handicapped people who were unable to shop. He had made several close friends and had also volunteered to take them to doctor's visits and other outings. Unfortunately, three of his closest friends, two men and a woman, had died.

He had also volunteered to mentor young children in schoolwork, serving as a volunteer tutor for several children whose English was not a first language. Although not fluent in Spanish, he did have enough mastery of the language to assist those children having difficulty in school. Since he had ample time on his hands, he had begun to read scientific journals and became interested in the electric universe. He sometimes felt that when he was describing his studies to people, he may have come across as somewhat eccentric. However, a large part of the electric universe was not theory but provable physical science. He was determined to organize his thoughts before he discussed his ideas with two very prominent religious scholars.

***

It was two minutes after six in the evening when Richard entered the lobby of the hotel. He immediately saw Naomi standing next to the concierge desk, talking to a woman. She smiled at him and said goodbye to the lady.

"Good evening, Richard," she greeted. "Right on time. I'm looking forward to dinner tonight with you and Jane."

"I am also very much looking toward our evening," he replied as he held the door to his car for her. After he had buckled up and started the car, he asked her for the address.

"It's 775 North Boundary Fence Drive, which, I am told, is north of Broadway, east of Houghton, and the nearest cross streets are Prairie View and Wood Chuck Way. I hope that helps."

"I know where it is," Richard replied as he entered the street and drove north toward Speedway. "It's about fifteen minutes from here."

"I didn't realize just how big Tucson is. Francine was telling me it's about forty miles from Vail on the southeast side to Marana on the northwest. It must be nice to have all this land to grow in."

"Well, we're packing them in. The Tucson metropolitan area has about one million people living here."

Naomi smiled as she glanced at him. He quickly turned toward her and returned the smile but quickly was back to concentrating on driving through what was the ending of Tucson's rush-hour traffic.

They spoke of the traffic and the weather, which had lately been ideal for January with daytime temperatures in the mid-sixties and the nighttime temperatures in the mid- to high thirties. When they arrived at the daughter's home, they walked to the front door together.

"Hello, please come in. I'm Rebecca, Jane's daughter. Mom is putting on her wrap and will be down in just a minute. May I offer you something?"

"No, thanks, honey. I'm Naomi Sverdlov, and this gentleman is Richard Valencia. We are both somewhat involved with your mother's participation in the roundtable discussion at the university."

"Yes! Mother told me about it. She is so excited to have been asked to participate. That young man sitting at the table, doing his homework, is my son, William. Unfortunately, my husband, Hunter, is still fighting his way through traffic. There was a minor emergency at work, and he had to stay a bit longer."

William smiled and waved as he looked up from his studies.

"Hello, everyone," he greeted.

Richard and Naomi waved back.

"It looks like you've got a lot on that table. What are you studying?" Naomi asked.

"Just high school algebra. It's a little work, but I think I'm getting it," William said.

"What does your husband do?" Naomi asked Rebecca.

"He works at Raytheon. He's an engineer there."

"I'm somewhat familiar with Raytheon," Richard said. "Some years ago, they were awarded the navy contract for manufacturing the 'Sharpshooter' long-range missile for the navy's Super Hornet."

"I believe so," Rebecca replied. "I really don't keep up with the details of Hunter's work since so much of it is classified, and I certainly don't want to inadvertently say something about his work that I shouldn't."

"Rebecca, Richard is also an engineer," Jane said as she entered the room. "Hello, Richard. I've heard about you from both Peter Glickman and Naomi. I am very much looking forward to hearing about your work."

"It's my pleasure, Jane. I too am looking forward to dining with such a distinguished scholar."

"Thank you, Richard, but it's you who I want to learn about."

"Have a good time, everyone. Mother, don't worry about time. We'll leave the light on."

CHAPTER FOUR

LA MAGDALENA RESTAURANT

Jane sat in the back seat behind Richard, so he could see her in the rearview mirror. She was an attractive woman of sixty-one years with just a few streaks of gray in her dark blond hair. He smiled as he glanced into the mirror and saw her blue eyes.

"Naomi tells me the name of the restaurant is La Magdalena. Is that true, Richard?"

"Yes. The restaurant bears the name of the barrio, or neighborhood that it is located in, Barrio Magdalena. It is one of the older barrios in Tucson, and many of the families there have been living there for generations."

"What a coincidence! One of my books was about Mary Magdalene. Have either of you heard of it?"

"Of course," Naomi answered. "As I recall, you referred to the Gospel of Mary one of the Nag Hammadi codices, which you so eloquently write about. Isn't it cited in that work that Mary Magdalene was Jesus's wife?"

"Many would answer that there is no concrete proof, Naomi, but I find the evidence compelling. Richard, I would be interested in what you think."

Richard looked into the rearview mirror for a second as he pulled into the parking lot of the restaurant.

"I believe the evidence is compelling, Jane. At least I believe that the evidence you cite in your book is compelling. Also, I'm a big fan of the World History Channel's religious history programs and believe other experts and scholars who believe as you do. Come, ladies, we can continue our conversation during dinner."

After they were seated and had ordered wine and dinner, the two ladies looked about them at the restaurant. Mexican "ranchero" music was playing in the background, somewhat more softly than Richard had remembered during his daytime dining trips. Several paintings on the wall of Mexico and Old Tucson were embellished by several black-and-white photographs of Tucson and her people of all races. The restaurant was nearly full with a variety of patrons, which included families, couples, and an assortment of other interesting people.

After dinner was served, Naomi remarked, "Richard, thank you for bringing us here. The ambiance is wonderful, the food is delicious, and the wine is perfect!"

"I agree," Jane added.

"Richard," Naomi said, "both Jane and I have read the draft you gave Dr. Glickman, but we would like you to give us your description of your thesis."

"I will. First, let's ask to be moved to the Arizona room. There are almost no diners in there. We will be able to speak without too much distraction."

CHAPTER FIVE

ORIGINS

After they were comfortably seated, Richard looked at his two companions, who smiled and looked back at him expectantly. He took a sip of wine and then leaned slightly forward in his seat.

"There was a circumstance on this planet when there was no time," he said. He paused to let his words enter his companions' consciousness. "At least what I call *human time* or that which is reckoned and measured by mankind. Whatever else time may be, its human concept arose at the origin of what has become our present-day solar system.

"The reason for that is there is a very cogent theory that originated with Velikovsky in his writings prior to publishing his first work, *Worlds in Collision*.[8] In those early writings, Velikovsky speculated that our planet Earth was part of a brown dwarf star system before it had been captured by our present solar system. The brown dwarf star was a binary system consisting of Saturn and Jupiter. This system also included the planets Venus, Mars, and Earth, locked in a configuration that kept the three planets in what I would describe as a straight-line array that rotated in synchronous movement or rotation around the two large planets, Saturn and Jupiter.

---

[8] Immanuel Velikovsky, *Worlds in Collision* (Garden City, New York: Doubleday & Company, Inc., 1950).

"The most benign situation for life in an electric universe is inside the electrical cocoon of a brown dwarf star. Radiant energy is then evenly distributed over the entire surface of any planet orbiting within the chromosphere of such a star, regardless of axial rotation, tilt, or orbital eccentricity. The exceedingly thin atmosphere of such stars has the essential water and carbon compounds to mist down onto planetary surfaces. The reddish light is ideal for photosynthesis.[9]

"I believe we don't know exactly how long this brown dwarf star system that Earth was part of existed before capture by our solar system, but it was probably for millions of years. I believe that it was in this system that life began and evolved and that humans existed in this system in what I would describe as an unconscious state. By unconscious state, I believe what Julian Jaynes described in his seminal work. The unconscious state was that of *the bicameral mind* or man's inability for introspection.[10] What I understand introspection to be is an act of self-awareness that involves thinking about and analyzing your own thoughts and behaviors and the ability to think about time in a linear way. This state of human evolution before introspection is what I think Jaynes believed was an unconscious state. That doesn't mean that humans weren't intelligent or not capable of cognition. I remember one of his examples is how we can perform familiar and perfunctory acts like driving a car. Sometimes when driving, we arrive at our destination without an acute memory of the events that transpired, as if we were on autopilot.

"My understanding of Jaynes's hypothesis is that man didn't evolve consciousness simply because his brain evolved into a more capable and complex organ until it reached critical mass

---

[9] Quoted from Wallace Thornhill and David Talbott, *The Electric Universe* (Portland, 2007).

[10] Julian Jaynes, *The Origin of Consciousness in the Breakdown of the Bicameral Mind* (Boston, New York: A Mariner Book Houghton Mifflin Company, 1976, 1973).

or became complex enough that it developed consciousness as a matter of evolution. I believe his thesis is that it was only after man developed language that he could develop the ability of consciousness or introspection.

"Julian Jaynes received his PhD in psychology from Yale and was a lecturer in psychology and consciousness in the Psychology Department at Princeton University. I was looking at the University of Arizona's catalogue not too long ago and was impressed at the curriculum for consciousness studies. It obviously is a complex subject, and I don't believe there is an agreement of its origin in humans yet. That's why I believe that Jaynes was at least on the right track. But I digress."

"Before you continue, I have a question," Naomi said.

"Sure. Please, what is it?" Richard responded.

"Maybe Jane is aware of a Harvard astronomer by the name of Harlow Shapely. Harlow was well known and respected in his field of astronomy and was one of the founders of the American Astronomical Society and the American Association for the Advancement of Science. He was also one of the founders of a campaign against Velikovsky's *Worlds in Collision* when it came out. I'm not sure if he referred to Velikovsky as a *crackpot* or if he merely agreed with those who did. I take it that you believe Velikovsky was not a crackpot?"

"I have heard of him. However, I didn't follow his work closely. I know it was highly respected, although there were some ideas that he got wrong, according to later developments," Jane answered.

"Not only do I not believe Velikovsky was a crackpot," Richard continued, "but I also believe he was one of the greatest thinkers of the twentieth century, equal to or even greater than Einstein. I do not know if Harlow Shapely ever called Velikovsky a crackpot. I do know that when asked why he believed events could not have happened as described by Velikovsky in his work, he said they could not have occurred according to the laws of

Newton. But what did Newton know about electricity?[11] Not much if anything. Both Newton and Shapely believed at the time that gravity was the sole force at work in the universe. This is understandable because it was one of the main assumptions that served as the basis not only for the modern view of cosmology but also even of Einstein's work. It is not true that gravity is the sole mover and shaker of the universe. The electromagnetic force is much greater than the force of gravity by a magnitude to the thirty-ninth power! As a matter of fact, of the known forces in what is termed the *standard model*—the strong nuclear force, the weak nuclear force, gravity, and the electromagnetic force—it is probable that they are all expressions of one force, which probably should be called the *electrostatic force.*

"What does all this have to do with the origin of religion?" Richard asked.

"I'm anxious to hear!" Jane replied.

"Think of Earth in this brown dwarf star system traveling through the galaxy until it came within the gravitational and electrical attraction of our solar system. This new force began to change the old configuration, the home of the birth of man and all living things on this planet, which was an ideal environment for life. It was in this benign environment that man evolved although with a nonintrospective mind. The forces exerted upon the brown dwarf system began to change. Man, emerging from the cocoon that was dimly lighted by the giant planet Saturn, was a living witness to the change, what he would describe as the *creation* in his later traditions of religion and myth. Among the changes was that of the electrical radiant cocoon. It began to disintegrate, slowly perhaps. We have no way of knowing for certain. These were *the waters of chaos* that Genesis speaks of. As it did, it revealed to observers on Earth the giant gas planet in the north, the planet Saturn. Originally, Jupiter, the other gas giant in this binary star system, was hidden behind Saturn.

---

[11] Wallace Thornhill and David Talbott, *The Electric Universe* (Portland, 2007).

Saturn was the first god of mankind. This was the creator, the benevolent god who had given mankind the golden age in which to peacefully evolve. This creation was remembered in many traditions of many people throughout the world. The Hebrew account of Genesis was one of many.

"As religious scholars, I believe both of you know that the Hebrew account of the creation was not the most ancient and was similar, if not, in part, based on the accounts of other ancient peoples.

"It is likely that the 'creation' recorded by ancient peoples was actually a fundamental change in the solar system. It may have lasted for hundreds, if not thousands, of years but the changes, although probably gradual at first, became more turbulent and violent to humans on earth who witnessed and lived through the changes. Some of the changes were cataclysmic catastrophes, which literally moved the earth on its foundation. To the ancient peoples on earth, who witnessed the changes and lived through the catastrophes, they were terrifying and life-changing events.

"Today scholars believe that Velikovsky made mistakes in some of his descriptions of what took place. For example, in *Worlds in Collision*, he states that in the fifteenth century BCE, Jupiter expelled a comet, which would become Venus. I mentioned above that when the brown dwarf binary star system was captured by our solar system, Venus was already a planet locked in a phased array around Saturn and Jupiter. Between Earth and Saturn were two other planets—Mars, closest to Earth, and between Mars and Saturn, the planet Venus. The perturbations caused by the capture of the system caused gravitational and electrical forces to disturb the system that had probably existed for millions of years, and the system began to change. It appears as if Jupiter and Saturn approached each other during an occlusion, which emitted a brilliant light witnessed by Earth's population and written about by Isaiah thousands of years later.[12] This is the probable ancient origin for the worldwide festival of lights celebrated around the world by many peoples during the winter solstice. It might have been during this process that Venus appeared to ancient observers to have been ejected from Saturn. But if Saturn was the origin of Venus, it happened prior to this time. It was also the cause of and inundation of water ejected from Saturn or Jupiter, which mankind remembers as the *deluge* or *flood* of Noah's time.[13]

"Venus became a flaming comet and passed close to Earth during the fifteenth century, which changed Earth's orbit and axial inclination, tilting Earth twenty-three degrees on its axis. This close pass caused many catastrophes, which became part of ancient observers' religious and or mythical traditions. Then according to Velikovsky, Venus passed close to Earth again some fifty-two years later, causing it to halt its rotation temporarily, resulting in further catastrophes with life-changing consequences. Velikovsky speculated that this might have been the origin of the Jubilee year and the smoking comet Venus may have been the origin of the long side curls worn by some observant Orthodox Jews.

"Velikovsky further documented that in the eighth and seventh centuries BCE, Mars, which had become displaced by Venus, passed close by Earth, causing further catastrophes. Eventually, after Mars's flybys, the solar system settled down into its current configuration. You can imagine the terror and fear experienced by those people on Earth who survived one or more of these catastrophes. They remembered them in their oral legends and later in their written traditions, and these traditions based on the cataclysmic events witnessed by mankind became the origin of not only his religion but his astronomy and astrology as well. It is in these traditions and memories that you

[12] Isaiah 30:26.

[13] Genesis 7:4, 10.

will find not only the origin of religion but also the origins of the archetypes discovered by Carl Gustav Jung in his work.[14]

"Very briefly, Jung's archetypes are those archaic patterns and images that are held deeply within the collective unconscious. To my knowledge, Jung never speculated exactly how the collective unconscious captured these archetypes. With our current knowledge of epigenetics, we have the biological and chemical knowledge to understand this process.

"That, briefly, is the background for my thesis on the origin of religion. I make no claims of research or of discovery of these facts but simply strive to correlate the work of others to enhance my understanding of the origin of religion. For me, my work will be the datum from which I intend to explore the origin of religion. I truly believe that you two religious scholars are eminently more qualified than I am to flesh out the details of religious thought and practice from the beginning of the emergence of man's consciousness to the complex and ultrasophisticated theology he has developed. I believe that in this knowledge, we can come to know the origin of religion, including the creation, the fall from heaven with its attendant original sin caused by Lucifer in the Garden of Eden, to the ritual and sacrifice we know today."

Jane looked at Richard with her wide eyes. He could not determine if she thought he was wrong or if something else was on her mind. Her eyes told him that she was concerned about something.

"Are you saying, Richard, that you are negating the traditional source of religious thought, at least in the West? Are you saying that revealed religion does not exist?"

"No, I'm not, Jane. When I first learned about revealed religion, it was in my Catholic catechism classes when I was young. It included everything from Moses receiving the Ten

---

[14] Carl Gustav Jung, *The Collected Works of C. G. Jung, volume 9, part 1* (Princeton, New Jersey: Princeton University Press, 1975).

Commandments on Mount Sinai to the fact that the pope is infallible in matters of religion because he is filled with the Holy Spirit.[15] I have come to realize that divine revelation may take other forms. For example, in our concept of the Almighty, one of the attributes that we acknowledge is *omniscience*. I'm not saying, nor do I believe any religion on the planet would presume to believe, that I or they understand God. However, in our limited human knowledge and understanding, it is logical to assume that omniscience would include the vehicle of knowing, and for us humans, that appears to be something similar to a mind. I believe that there is a scientific case to be made for what appears to be telepathy and human transference among human minds. I believe there is also a case to hypothesize that it may have been more prevalent in ancient man as a survival tool and that we have lost some of its use. If that is the case, or even if it's only a viable hypothesis, then how much more capable would it be for the Almighty to reveal to human minds knowledge or religious truth?"

"Richard! Richard!" Naomi looked first at Jane and then at him. "I believe I am beginning to understand where you are coming from. You're not making an attack on religion per se but are seeking to establish a historical perspective, for yourself initially but certainly of benefit to those of us who are vitally interested in religious thought. I think that is a worthy goal, and I am proud of you for undertaking such a difficult task. I don't mean to speak for Jane. She is eminently qualified to think and speak for herself, but I believe she would agree that there are many *entrées* into religion. I don't have to believe in the Mormon religion to perhaps understand the concept or experience of revelation Joseph Smith received when he found the golden plates in New York revealed to him by the Angel Moroni. In the final analysis, religion is a human endeavor because

---

[15] "He who hears you hears me" (Luke 10:16); "Whatever you bind on earth shall be bound in heaven" (Matt. 18:18).

without humans on planet Earth, there would be no religion. I do not believe that all religions are equal or that there is only one true religion. I believe that religious thought originates from human understanding, and if we must presume that human understanding comes from spiritual and mental intercourse with the Almighty, then it becomes mankind's struggle to connect with the divine as it seems right to him.

"Jane is a devout Christian, and I've read her account of how her faith has helped her through difficult times. I have similar experiences when my faith guided me through extremely difficult times. I even remain a devout Jew knowing full well that modern archeology in general and Israeli archeology in particular have pretty much determined that there was no massive Exodus of Jews from Egypt or a wandering in the desert for forty years with a tribe that would have probably numbered several hundred thousand people or more, not including livestock and baggage. There is simply no record of such a wandering. It is a central core of the Jewish faith, and it doesn't matter to me if it didn't historically exist. What matters is that it is a core tenant of my faith, and in the final analysis, religion is a belief system by those who seek the divine."

Jane looked at Richard with what he thought was understanding and perhaps even affection in her eyes.

"I agree with Naomi, Richard. I believe that you are not a *deist* who doesn't believe in revealed religion but who relies on reason and knowledge of its design and laws. Of course, if there is *design* in nature, that belief does imply a *designer*. I believe that you, as Naomi and me, are at the least a theist, someone who believes that the Creator reveals Himself to mankind through various ways. Not all theists do, of course, and there are many kinds of theists, including pantheists, monotheists, and polytheists. That being said, I understand that religion is an attempt by humans to seek and understand their role with the divine. Religion is as much a cultural tradition as it is religious belief. I also believe that in the final analysis, each of us will make his or her choice based on belief, faith, and religious motivation. By religious motivation, I mean the desire to understand our place in the universe and to strive to achieve it.

"I know Naomi had translated ancient texts that reveal that a Semitic people speaking Hebrew left large jars at Kuntillet Ajrud in the northwest of the Arabian Peninsula or Southwestern Sinai with written reference in early Hebrew to Yahweh and his Asherah or one of the gods of Israel and his consort or wife. These were but two deities of that tribe that included several other deities similar to those in contemporary times to other peoples of the Middle East. The struggle toward monotheism for Jews was a long and tedious one and may not have been accepted as cannon until the sixth century BCE under the political drive for reunification of Israel under the king of Judah, Josiah. The Bible, or Torah, and the New Testament are a written testimony of man's struggle to believe in the divine."

Naomi said, "I have to say that one of the tenets of Orthodox Judaism is that not only was the Tanakh given to Moses on Mount Sinai but the entire oral and written commentary as well. Reform Judaism, as you know, Richard, believes only the Tanakh was given. I personally believe as the Reform Jews do. There is a well-known story in the *Tractate Shabbat*[16] about Hillel. A so-called heathen approached Hillel and asked Hillel to teach him the entire Torah while standing on one foot. Hillel replied to the effect, 'What is hateful to you do not do to your neighbor: that is the whole Torah while the rest is commentary; go and learn it.'

"Of course, we all know that the temple and sacrifice by the priest was the core of Judaism until the temple was destroyed and the Israelites scattered. It was then that Rabbinic Judaism evolved to ensure the continuity of belief and proper understanding of the scriptures. Now I agree that the Exodus from Egypt, as described in the Tanakh, is likely apocryphal, but there is a basis

---

[16] The Talmud in *Tractate Shabbat*, 31.

in legend for its origin. Perhaps it was something in the heavens that ancient man witnessed as you have so eloquently told us."

"I repeat," Richard responded, "you two religious scholars are eminently more qualified to trace the development of religion than I. For me, it is a personal quest more so than a scholarly one. Therefore, if you care to contribute your knowledge and scholarship to my work, I would be grateful."

Naomi smiled at him and spoke. "'Sh'ma Yisrael, Adonai Eloheinu, Adonai Echad. Hear, O Israel, the Lord is our God, the Lord is One. The Lord of Hosts; the Queen of Heaven.' These epithets and others like them have always been appellations given to the divine on Judaism's long struggle toward monotheism. I agree with you that Velikovsky's work may shed light on the origins."

"Tell me, Naomi or Richard, the answer to this question: why did Moses return from the mountain to discover that the Jews had built a golden bull to worship? I have yet to hear a good explanation for the quick turn to idolatry," Jane asked.

"I can try," Richard said. "To get a clearer understanding, I recommend you read *Worlds in Collision* or *The Saturn Myth* by Talbott.[17] I believe you will come to understand a very reasonable hypothesis for many concepts in the Bible and other religions' traditions. Remember, to the ancients, these beliefs were not myths but reality based on a perspective that did not distinguish between religion and science.

"According to Velikovsky and Talbott, when the waters of chaos separated, mankind could look to the northern skies and see the planet Saturn, which was the first god of religious or mythical tradition. At night, Saturn appeared as a prodigiously large globe but did reflect sunlight from our present sun. I say present sun because when Saturn manifested itself to the peoples of Earth, they considered it the original sun or the

---

[17] David Talbott, *The Saturn Myth* (Garden City, New York: Doubleday & Company, Inc., 1980).

sun of night. Much as the crescent moon reflects sunlight not blocked by Earth, so did Saturn reflect a crescent at midnight. Because Saturn appeared as such an enormous globe, the crescent at midnight was at its lower region, or bottom, and appeared to those on Earth as the golden horns of a giant bull. That is another epithet of the divine in ancient times, *The Bull of Heaven*. The crescent would appear to move around Saturn as the sun changed its position relative to the configuration Earth was in at the time. It was brightest at midnight, on the bottom, and weakest at noon on top. That, by the way, is probably why many ancient calendars, including the Jewish, began the day at sundown. That is when the golden crescent was most prominent in the heavens. So the Jews became frightened by the sound and lightning that emanated from Mount Sinai when Moses was there and, in their fear, built the golden calf probably because it was a familiar object of worship from ancient times among all peoples."

Richard glanced at his wrist watch; it was 11:30 p.m. Because he was driving, Richard had limited himself to one glass of wine. His two companions, animated by the discussion of religion, had had four glasses each, and Richard realized it was time to end the discussion and take his companions home.

"Naomi, Jane, thank you for a truly enjoyable evening. I hope that you have enjoyed our discussion as much as I have. The hour is late, and I believe it's best to go home."

"Richard! You have no idea how much I've enjoyed this evening. I certainly have a good idea of what I'll be reading in the immediate future. I realize that much of what you told us tonight comes from the work of others, but your willingness to try to understand previous efforts and bring order to a wide spectrum of research and knowledge has greatly motivated me to learn more," Jane said.

"I also will have a lot to look forward to on my return to Israel, which, by the way, I almost regret to say, will be in three days. Richard, I am amused by what you said about not having an advanced degree. You certainly speak with a great deal of knowledge and research. I too have thoroughly enjoyed this evening, so much so that I am tempted to try to continue into the wee hours of the morning. However, I do have a nine-o-clock meeting tomorrow to begin to wrap up the discussion with Glick and his colleagues. I agree. It's time to go." Naomi smiled at him as she spoke.

"Let me take care of the bill, and we'll be on our way. Jane, we will drop you off first if that is OK?"

"Yes, of course, Richard," she answered.

CHAPTER SIX

SHALOM

Richard walked Naomi back to her hotel room. She gently kissed him on his lips and smiled. "Thank you for a lovely night. I thoroughly enjoyed myself. Listen, I don't want this night to end just yet. I'll be returning back to Israel in a few days, and I don't want to rush any goodbyes. Why don't you come in and we'll chat for a while?"

"Thanks, Naomi. Please let me know when you're tired. You've been extremely busy and have an obligation tomorrow."

"You've got a deal. Listen, sit on the sofa over there. I'll pour us another glass of wine."

Richard did as she asked and accepted a glass of Merlot. She set her glass on the end table next to the couch.

"Excuse me for a minute while I use the ladies' room."

Richard sipped his wine while he remembered their evening together. He had given her the last information on his thesis, and she seemed genuinely captivated by it. She had told him that he had inspired her to further study Velikovsky and the electric universe. He smiled when he thought of her comment that she was going to be busy when she returned to Israel, presumably to pursue her new interest in the origin of religion.

After several minutes and several sips of wine, Richard felt mellow with a warm glow of contentment that suffused through him.

"Are you doing OK?" she asked as she returned, picked her glass, and sat next to him.

"Yes, I am. Thanks," he replied with a smile.

"Stand up," she said as she put her glass down and stood.

He did as she said. She came close to him, put her arms around his neck, and gently kissed him. Richard felt a surge of desire overcome him as he held her. He could feel her sweet, warm breath and her breasts close to him. He kissed her, and she responded with a lingering soft kiss, her lips pressed gently against his for several minutes.

"Come," she said. She took his hand and led him into the bedroom.

They made love with a gentle passion that lingered during the night. Naomi softly verbalized her pleasure several times. When the light of dawn entered the hotel room, she fell asleep in his arms with him lying behind her and embracing her.

When the eight-o-clock hour arrived, he gently released her from his embrace and slowly started to get out of bed. She awakened with a smile.

"Good morning, Richard. What a beautiful night."

"Naomi, I will never forget you. I hope we will have an opportunity to meet again."

"Come to Israel, Richard. You may have a future there."

"I'm not sure of what I could do. I'm certainly not a scholar."

"You'd be surprised. It would be enough to be with me. It would be enough to be together."

"I've always wanted to return, but I never could bring myself to do it since I lost Rachel."

She looked at him with an expression in her eyes that made him understand she felt his loss.

"I understand, Richard, as someone who has also suffered loss. It usually wouldn't matter when or where two people would share their life, but Israel is my destiny no matter what the future may bring."

"I understand, Naomi. I do."

He did not see her again before she departed for Israel two days later. They said their goodbyes over the telephone, and he promised he would make a sincere attempt to see her again in Israel.

"Richard, you can gain a much better understanding of the origins about which you speak and write in the Holy Land. Perhaps when you come, you will decide to stay, if not forever but as long as you are content. I believe you will be content with me. I know I will."

It was difficult to speak because of the emotion that engulfed him.

"I just may, Naomi. I won't make a promise now, but when the time comes, I'll call you."

"That's good enough for me. Shalom."

"Shalom, Naomi," he answered.

CHAPTER SEVEN

TEXAS FIDDLES

Jane had called him several times after her involvement with the round table came to an end. During one of the conversations, she had mentioned that she had been craving a steak dinner. Richard told her he would take her to a good restaurant and kept his promise. He picked her up at the front door. Rebecca and the family were not home. They drove to the Georgia Peach Restaurant and Steak House on the Old Spanish Trail about ten miles east of Tucson. He had eaten there several times during the week, so he was surprised when he saw that live music was offered.

"That's an unusual name," Jane said. "I wonder what the origin of it is."

"The back of the menu has a little history. Georgia and her husband moved here from Savannah, Georgia, about fifteen years ago for his health and opened this restaurant. According to the bio on the back, they fell in love with the Southwest and decided on the Western theme. You'll find lots of paintings and photographs of cowboys, cattle, horses, and rodeo scenes on the walls. Her husband, Bob, passed away about two years ago, and she runs the restaurant now with the help of her two sons."

"My," Jane said as he opened the door for her, "it sounds as if there's a party going on."

"I've been here a few times for their vaquero steak but somehow always during the week. It makes sense they would offer live entertainment during the weekend."

They entered the Western-themed restaurant and were seated by the young hostess, who took their order for Cabernet Sauvignon and steaks.

The band was returning from a break, and the leader advised the crowd that the next number was a favorite of Georgia and several patrons who had requested it. "We have two of the best fiddle players in Tucson who are about to back our vocalist, Sally. Please welcome Sally."

The crowd applauded quietly, and the two fiddles filled the room with Texas-style music.

Richard smiled at Jane as she seemed fascinated by the total scene. Her eyes twinkled as she said, "Richard, please, let's dance."

"Of course!" he replied.

There were five other couples on the dance floor as he held her in his arms, and they began to move to the music. She was remarkably light on her feet, and he soon realized she was an excellent dancer. He began to lead her through some dance moves he had learned with Cathy while they were dating and had gone to several country dances outside of Savannah. It was as if Jane could anticipate his next move. Most of the couples danced in the middle of the floor, but Richard and Jane moved around the perimeter several times, often reversing from a clockwise to a counterclockwise pattern. Frequently, she would look up at him and smile. Her eyes expressed the joy she felt. The twin Texas fiddles were a perfect segue into a subtle shift from the present into an enchanted feeling for the two of them. She was again a beautiful young woman enthralled in her partner's arms, flowing easily to the rhythm and soul of the music, which spoke of faded love, loneliness, and hope for new love with a passion softened by tenderness. The music eloquently sung of a youthful lust for life and love in a rural world where the future was limitless and shared love was the core of happiness. He was grateful to hold her close to him as they moved as one to the music.

After they had returned to their table and were served, she remarked, "Richard, you are a wonderful dancer. I thoroughly enjoyed myself dancing with you. After dinner, we must try it again."

"Thank you, Jane. You are kind. The highest compliment I've ever received about my dancing is that "It was OK . . .""

After they had eaten, she said, "You are much too modest, even with your work in progress. You certainly have a very interesting and compelling thesis about the origin of religion. I am fascinated by it."

"As I've mentioned several times, none of my work is original. I am merely trying to gather and correlate some very brilliant and hard work that others have done."

"Of course, you are. I see you're finished. I'll ask for a box to take the rest of this wonderful steak home. It was delicious! Come, let's dance some more before they take another break."

During one of Sally's vocals, he felt Jane hold him more closely. He thought that she was enjoying not only the country music but also the words that drifted over the dance floor. He glanced down at her. Her eyes were closed, and she seemed to be lost in thought.

A few minutes before eleven o'clock, Jane advised him that she was beginning to tire.

"Although my cancer is in remission, I'm still not fully recovered from the chemo. I'm still undergoing physical therapy to regain my strength. This is about the most enjoyable physical therapy I've had yet. Thanks for a wonderful dinner and evening."

"Thank you, Jane. Believe me when I tell you how much I've enjoyed myself. I'll take you home now."

"Richard," she said, "Rebecca and Hunter took William to Greer up in the White Mountains. Hunter is teaching William how to fly-fish. They rented a cabin there for five days, and they won't be home until tomorrow afternoon. I'm all alone for a while. Perhaps we can go to your place and you can offer me another glass of wine while I rest."

When they arrived at Richard's home, he and Jane entered the living room.

"This is a nice home, Richard. I would like to see the drive during the day. We are close to the mountains, are we not?" Jane asked.

"Yes. A few years after Rachel passed, I sold our home. It was perfect for raising a family but a little too big for just me. I purchased this town house away from the city. It has only two bedrooms, but I did have a two-bedroom, two-bath guesthouse built. It was specifically for my children and grandchildren to visit. I have a feeling I should have made it a three bedroom. I am expecting more grandchildren in the future."

"Expecting? Is it your daughter or son?"

"I may be putting the cart before the horse. Michael wrote me a letter that his tour of duty in Iraq is over and after he reports at his new command at Fort Bragg, he will be returning to Tucson to visit me while on thirty days' leave. I am very happy to be able to see him soon but even happier because I suspect the main reason he is coming home is to reintroduce me to the woman he will formally propose to. He's mentioned in his letter that he wants to start a family with her. So I am confident that there may be some new grandchildren in my future!"

"Reintroduce? I assume you've met her before."

"Yes. She's a wonderful girl. Her name is Shura Vega. Michael met her while they were both students here at the university. She was here on a student's visa. She was born and raised in Mexico City. She is a Sephardic Jew by birth, although I remember that after they became serious about his junior year, she started attending our reform synagogue. Rachel and she liked each other very much. I suspect Rachel would be pleased."

"Isn't it a little unusual for a Jewish girl to be from Mexico? Also, where is she now?"

"She is leaving Iraq for Israel then to Tucson to meet Michael before she returns to Mexico City, where her family lives. Michael told me in his letter that he has informally proposed to her but will do it formally here in Tucson with a ring and an announcement, I think. I'm not sure, but I suspect her family will have to be involved. We'll just wait and see, I suppose.

"There is a Jewish community in Mexico City as well as other cities in the country. She had previously told us that in Mexico City, there are several communities, including Ashkenazi Jews from various parts of Europe, and two distinct Syrian communities, one from Aleppo and one from Damascus. Of course, there is still a community of Jews that date from the conquest or during Spain's rule where the community was almost entirely Sephardic Jews from that nation. According to Shura, the Jewish community is very close knit, and intermarriage between Jews and non-Jews is extremely rare. If you meet Shura, you will come to know that she is a woman that is not constrained by social norms. She is not only adventurous but also constantly seeking knowledge of the world around her. It is rare for people of the community there, especially of women, to seek wider horizons."

"That is interesting. Promise me that you will tell me more about Michael and Shura later. Right now, I would like to share a glass of wine with you. I had a wonderful evening. I haven't felt this good or this young in quite a while."

They sat together on the couch and sipped their wine while they talked for an hour or so. They spoke of their past, their deceased spouses and family, their careers, and their hope for the future. They also spoke of the impending death that grew ever closer as they aged. Richard sensed that Jane was becoming fond of him as he was of her. He also sensed a feeling that she needed him to be with her.

"Jane," he said, "if you would like to spend the night, you can sleep in my bed, and I will sleep in the guest bedroom. I can take you home tomorrow whenever you wish."

"Richard, being with you has awakened a need for tenderness in me that only you can fill. Please take me to bed." She smiled at him while standing and placing her arms around his neck. She then kissed him with a tenderness that belied her underlying passion.

When they entered the bedroom, Jane did not leave for the bathroom but undressed in front of him slowly and deliberately, gently folding and placing her clothes on the recliner next to the window while always looking at him. She smiled as she lifted the sheet and slowly lay down with the sheet covering her breasts while she waited expectantly for him to join her.

He did so, taking a cue from her demeanor to approach her gently and with as much tenderness as possible. They softly kissed each other with gentle, lingering kisses that slowly filled him with an overwhelming desire to love her.

Throughout the night, their lovemaking was complete and passionate but yet gentle and tender. Although not verbal, Jane would grasp his arms when she was fulfilled with a strength that surprised him.

Richard had no idea what time it was when Jane softly slipped into slumber with his arms around her, her back to him. When he heard her soft, steady breathing, indicating she was asleep, he permitted himself to sleep. It was a night he would never forget.

It was nine o'clock when Jane awakened. Richard had been up since seven.

"That coffee smells wonderful," Jane said from the bedroom as she dressed.

"Good morning! I can have breakfast ready in a few minutes. Would you like eggs, toast, bacon, or sausage? Or if you desire, I can whip up a batch of pancakes."

"I'm famished this morning. How about scrambled eggs, bacon, sausage, and toast to go with my coffee?"

"You've got it. I'll pour your coffee now. There's cream and sugar on the table if you need."

"So you don't keep kosher?" Jane asked over breakfast.

"Rachel started out observing kashruth, but when the kids came, she still abided by the law, but with so many items certified kosher by the five agencies here in the States, she deferred to their judgment. She always stated that although she loved her Jewish faith, she would do whatever was necessary for our marriage. It wasn't a problem. I loved her cooking whatever it was, and the times I prepared meals, I was careful to follow the guidelines, especially as a teaching tool for the children.

"Jane, I don't know if I've mentioned this to you before, but I have never been what I consider to be a pious or observant Catholic or Jew. Rachel was aware of that and had no problem, especially since I converted and we raised both our children as Jews. They even underwent Orthodox conversion in our reform synagogue to ensure their acceptance if they ever needed it."

When it was time to leave, Jane marveled at the Catalina mountain range, which seemed so close to Richard's town house.

"Rebecca called me on my cell phone while I was in the bedroom. They returned earlier than anticipated because Hunter received a call from his work about some crisis that needed his attention. They left yesterday evening and arrived around midnight instead of leaving this morning and returning in the afternoon. I had left a note that I was going out with you, so when she returned home, she called me to ensure I was OK. I told her that not only was I OK but also felt better than I had for some time."

"I can understand how she would be worried coming home and finding her mother missing."

"I've told Rebecca that I was the worried mom when she was growing up. Now our roles are somewhat reversed. She's the one who worries about me. I'm not usually such a free spirit, but with you, I feel like I can fly again."

Richard smiled as he drove her home.

Rebecca greeted them at the door and invited Richard in to meet her husband. He noticed that she gave her mother a wide-eyed, curious look.

"Richard, this is my husband, Hunter. Hunter, this gentleman is Richard Valencia, a friend of Mother."

"It is a pleasure to meet you, sir," Hunter said as he shook Richard's hand. "I've heard quite a bit about you from both Rebecca and Jane."

"I hope some of it's good," Richard replied with a smile.

"Don't worry, Richard," Rebecca said as she beckoned him to enter the living room and sit next to Jane on the couch. "Mother, you seemed to have enjoyed yourself while we were gone."

"Absolutely! Richard treated me to a wonderful steak dinner and wine, but even more enjoyable is that we danced almost every dance after we ate until I started to get tired. Even then, I didn't want to quit."

"Your mother is an exceptional dancer. She enjoyed herself with me, and I make no claims to be a good dancer."

"Well, before Mother settled on her major, she had intended to study dance with the intent of performing. I myself believe that you are a good dancer, Richard, but even if you weren't, Mother would still make you look good. Mother, I haven't seen you this happy in quite a while. Whatever Richard and you are doing, it's working quite well. I hope you two keep it up."

It seemed to Richard that Rebecca was about to say more, but the look and smile from Jane was enough to keep her quiet. Richard thought that maybe the two women would talk in private when the men, including William, were not present.

Hunter was leaving to go to work to resolve whatever crisis brought the family back early to Tucson. Richard took advantage of his leaving to make his departure.

After he had said farewell, Rebecca started to walk him to the door.

"Thanks, Becky," Jane told her. "I'll walk him to his car."

When they were at his car, Jane took both of his hands and kissed him.

"Adios, Richard," she told him. "Adios but not goodbye. Go with God and be safe. I hope we will see each other again and sooner rather than later. When I lost John, I was prepared to spend the rest of my life alone. It was enough for me to dedicate myself to my work and my daughter. Now I realize that I have a need I hadn't really accepted until last night. I do not mean to seem forward or that I'm trying to impose myself on you. We are both mature adults who have each lived full lives with many others with whom we loved. I want you to know that I am terribly fond of you and I would like very much to continue to see you frequently. Do you understand?"

"Yes, I do. I promise we will spend more time together. Take care of yourself, and I will call you soon."

She kissed him again and then turned toward the house. Richard followed her with his eyes and noticed Rebecca looking at them from the window.

He smiled and waved goodbye.

CHAPTER EIGHT

JANET COLLINS

Richard and Jane stopped at the Good Brew Coffee Shop, a small and quiet enclave in the busy Tucson Mall with over fifty varieties of coffee to choose from. Jane had asked Richard to take her shopping at the electronics store in the mall. Her grandson William's birthday was next week, and she wanted to surprise him with a laptop computer to replace his small and limited tablet that he had been using for two years.

They had enjoyed several excursions together recently. Some were for shopping, some for lunch, some to attend lectures together at the University of Arizona's lecture series at Centennial Hall. Sometimes it was just a quiet walk in the park when the weather was nice. They had been spending more time together with the enthusiastic but quiet approval of Rebecca.

Jane waited for him at a small table in a quiet corner of the shop while he ordered and returned with two cups of coffee and a large slice of banana cake with two plastic forks. Just as he sat, Richard's cell phone rang. He did not recognize the number, so he sat the phone on the table with the speaker on so Jane could listen in. It seemed somewhat rude for him to answer his phone while they were continuing a conversation and enjoying coffee together.

"Hello, this is Richard," he answered.

"Richard Valencia, I assume?" the female voice on the other end asked.

Richard could see Jane's face illuminate her curiosity.

"Yes. Do I know you?"

"No, sir, but I know of you. We have a mutual friend, Dr. Peter Glickman. Do you know him?"

"Yes." Richard wasn't sure what the woman was after, so his answer was noncommittal.

"My name is Janet Collins. I have known Dr. Glickman for about two years. He has given several speeches to the AAA of which I am a member. About two months ago, he gave me a copy of a draft of a book that you're working on about the origin of religion. Are you still there?"

"Yes. Are you a member of the American or Arizona Automobile Association?" Richard asked, puzzled.

"No!" She laughed. "The AAA I am a member of is the Arizona Atheists Association. Please don't be shocked. I can explain. The president of the Arizona Atheists Association chapter here in Tucson is Aaron Silver, MD. He is a neurosurgeon at the University of Arizona Hospital. As a result, we hold our chapter meetings and lectures or seminars in a small auditorium in the hospital."

"Is it small because you don't have many members?" Richard asked with a wink at Jane.

Janet laughed. "No. You'd be surprised at the number of atheists and secular humanist Jews there are in Tucson. Dr. Silver is affiliated with both organizations. But the reason I called is that Dr. Glickman mentioned a book you're working on about the origin of religion. He piqued my interest. When he seemed to forget about it, I called him and asked if I could pick it up at his office. He readily agreed and even made a copy of it for me. While reading it, I received an epiphany. I was so enthralled that I read it several times. I then obtained copies of *Worlds in Collision* and *The Saturn Myth* and spent numerous hours on several electric universe websites."

Janet paused speaking. Jane spoke softly to Richard. "That does not surprise me. I believe your book will have a similar effect on several people who read it."

"Oh, I'm sorry. I hope I didn't interrupt something. I heard a lady speaking to you about how she is not surprised that your draft had an effect on me."

Richard looked at Jane, who softly said, "It's not a problem at all."

"The lady I'm with and whose voice you heard is a very prominent scholar of religious history who has published several highly regarded books about religion, especially about Christianity. She seems to be as interested about the purpose of your call as I am. Can you please enlighten us?"

"Yes, I would love to meet both of you and discuss your work. Briefly, I'll give some of my background. I am currently a registered nurse here at the hospital and am working on a master's degree. It is my intent to someday work with the missions in Africa run by an association of Evangelical Protestant churches. That may sound strange to you, but long story short, I was raised in a very strict religious family of a local congregation called the Church of Christ's Covenant. I considered myself a normal girl with a desire to live and experience life as fully as possible. It seemed that I was doomed to damnation no matter what I did unless I adhered to a rigid code of morality. I tried my best to comply and did so, albeit not very well, until college when I began to learn about other people and their beliefs. It was a lengthy journey, but I eventually lost all religious faith and became an avowed atheist. My impetus for that loss was what I consider to be religious superstition and hatred by those fearful of other people who don't believe as they do. It didn't help when I informed my parents that I was lesbian.

"Your work has opened up a new hope for me that I can begin to learn about the origin of religion. It's like being able to find the cause of a disease so one can begin to work on a cure."

"Richard," Jane said, "can I ask Janet a question?"

"Janet, the lady I'm with is Jane. She would like to ask you a question. Is that OK?"

"Yes!" Janet replied.

Richard handed Jane the phone.

"Janet, you said that you were raised in a very religious fundamentalist family. Why, may I ask, do you seek to work in their missions in Africa?"

"Because, Jane, the people of my family's church are good people who seek to follow the religious teachings of Christ and seek not only to spread the gospel but also to alleviate suffering and poverty in the world. I don't have to believe their teachings to know that they do good work. The church is a vehicle for me to also do what I believe is good and right. It gives a higher purpose to my life."

"I believe you are not only a very intelligent woman but a good one is well. Just because I am a religious Christian does not mean I don't believe that God speaks to us all through different ways. I believe He is speaking to you whether you believe in Him or not."

"Thank you, ma'am. I hope I get to meet you as well as Richard, and perhaps we can have a discussion. I have been sincerely moved by Richard's work and the fact that his work has led me to a vast resource of knowledge about the origin of religion not only through science but through archeology and history as well. I won't take up any more of your time. Please let me speak to Richard, and I'll give him my number. If he, or the two of you, agrees to meet with me, he can call me when it's convenient."

"Yes. I would like to speak with you again, Janet. Goodbye. Here's Richard."

After Richard had entered Janet's phone number into his cell phone, he said, "Janet, let me check my schedule. I'm expecting my son to return to Tucson soon, so I may be busy. I promise I'll call you and we'll get together. Is that OK?"

"Yes! Thank you. I'll be waiting for your call. Goodbye."

"Goodbye."

"Wow," Richard said, "I certainly didn't expect anything like that. What do you think?"

"Richard, I have to admit when I heard her voice, initially, I felt a twinge of emotion I hadn't experienced for years, and I even enjoyed it to some extent."

"What was that?"

"Just a brief feeling of jealousy until I heard her say she was a lesbian. Isn't that silly?"

He smiled at her as he reached across the table and took her hand in his.

"Jane, I am very grateful to be able to be with you and share time together."

CHAPTER NINE

RETURN TO TUCSON

Richard was just finishing up the breakfast dishes when the home phone rang. He knew it was a long-distance call because of the double ring.

"Hello," he answered.

"Dad, this is Michael! How are you?"

"I'm fine, Michael. The question is, how you are? Where are you?"

"I'm here in New York City. I flew up yesterday from Fayetteville and got a hotel room for a few days. I'll be meeting Shura at JFK International Airport later this morning. She'll be arriving from Tel Aviv, and I'll be waiting for her after she clears customs. It took her a couple of days to receive her visa for the United States. She has both an Israeli and a Mexican passport because of her dual citizenship. She was told there may be a small problem clearing customs because both of her passports have Iraqi border crossing stamps on them. Homeland Security Personnel will probably want to interview her.

"We'll spend a few days here in New York City. We plan on taking in a couple of Broadway shows and hitting some restaurants that we've both been planning to eat at if we ever got the chance. Well, now we have that chance. After that, I've booked reservations on a direct flight to Tucson. When did Tucson start offering direct flights to and from New York City?"

"I'm not sure. I believe I read something about it in the local paper but didn't catch the details."

"No matter, I'm glad. We'll be spending only a few days in Tucson, just long enough to get reacquainted with you and contact some friends. Some of Shura's friends from the university are still there as are some of mine and even a few mutual friends from when we were dating. After those few days, we'll be heading to Mexico City to meet her parents and family and to formally announce our engagement."

"After that, what are your plans, Michael? Where will you be married?"

"That remains to be seen. I believe you know that Shura is from a traditional Orthodox Sephardic family. I don't think they will cotton too well to the idea of having her marriage anywhere other than Mexico City. You may have to book a flight and maybe Sarah and her family as well. I'll try to hold out for a marriage here in Tucson, but I have to tell you, Dad, I'm not that optimistic."

"I understand, Michael. Don't worry about it. Listen, don't be shy. All this traveling and wedding expense is going to cost you a pretty penny. Don't hesitate about letting me know if you need some financial assistance. Can I ask you a question?"

"Sure."

"What did Shura's family think of her not only joining the Israeli army but also traveling to Iraq to join the Peshmerga? I heard that it's a violation of Israeli law to do so."

"You can probably guess that it was a shock followed by an even greater shock. Her father has had more difficulty accepting her actions than her mother, who, according to Shura, has resigned herself to her daughter's independence. She once told Shura that she wished she would have named her Deborah after one of the seven women judges of Israel. Shura's mother Raquel is herself named after the Rachel in the Torah. She prides herself in always working to be a Jewish woman of worth as celebrated in

Eshet Chayil.[18] Shura told me that's why it is easier for her mother to accept her daughter's nontraditional behavior."

"You've got me there, son. Remember, I didn't have the advantage of attending Hebrew school like you as a youngster. What is the *Eshet Chayil*?"

"Sorry, Dad. Throughout Jewish history, women have been celebrated as the foundation of the home for keeping a kosher home, bringing up the children and keeping the atmosphere in the home conducive to Torah and mitzvoth. In her family, it is traditional for the men to sing the hymn to their women after Shul when they come home to the candles, welcoming them with light and warmth. I knew of several families in Israel who do that, and according to what Shura has told me, many Sephardic families in her community do so as well. The reason that her mother jokes that she should have named her Deborah is not only for Deborah's leadership and wisdom as a judge of Israel but also for her valor in battle. I believe Shura told me that the tradition originated with the Cabalists in the seventeenth century, who viewed Shabbat as a mystical union with the divine. They understood the hymn to be an allegory for the Shechinah, the feminine presence of God. I know you are familiar with Proverbs 31."

"Not the hymn, which I will certainly read. This brings up a good point, son. There is a topic that I would like to discuss with you when you're here if you have time."

"Can you give me a brief summary of what it is?"

"It's a book that I am putting together of significant research and work by several scholars in a pursuit to explore the origin of religion. I started this project solely for my own purpose of trying to better understand why religion is such a strong force in

---

[18] A woman of valor; consists of the concluding section of the book of Proverbs (31:10–31) sung on Friday night by traditional families praising the wife and mother.

humans. It's complex, but there is light at the end of the tunnel because of the hard work of many in various fields."

"You're right. I would love to sit down with you and discuss it at length, maybe even work with you in some capacity. Right now, I'm up to my ass in alligators. You know, Dad, you've always been honest with others about your religious conviction. Mother was the devout one in the family, but even she had a pretty good understanding and accepted the diversity of other people's beliefs. I think I fall in somewhere between you and Mom, although war has left a bitter taste in my mouth. I have not really come to terms with it. I can tell you that Shura will keep and celebrate her faith and teach our children in the Jewish way. I believe that's true even after her years of being a soldier and seeing the world through a soldier's eyes. I think that is the reason she is not even close to being what I would call devout and pious. She has always told me she can be observant while keeping a broad perspective of humanity. She is an amazing person."

"I agree. I know you're busy, so I won't keep you too long, but remember what I said about financial assistance."

"I will, Dad. Thanks. Don't forget as a bachelor, I've been receiving my regular army pay for several years now, and that's not including special pay and hazardous duty pay with its income tax breaks. I'm doing OK. I mean, my needs are not extravagant, and I've been socking away quite a bit. But I appreciate your offer, and if I get a little short, I may ask for a loan from you."

"Promise you won't hesitate. I'm glad that you're well and healthy. You are not in one of the safest professions, you know."

"I know. Dad, there is one favor both Shura and I would like to ask from you."

"Please, Michael, ask."

"We would both like to visit Mother's grave. Then we would like to attend services with you to ensure a minyan and say Kaddish. It is still not seven years since Mother's passing, and her Yahrzeit will be when we're in Tucson."

"Yes, of course. I'll ensure that it happens. Would you like a rabbi to accompany us to her grave?"

"No, just the three of us or anyone else you want to accompany you. By the way, it's been six years since Mom passed. Have you done any dating yet?"

"Nothing serious or steady. I'm still not ready or interested. I do have several woman friends whom I enjoy being with. Before I forget, I definitely want you two to stay with me. Either you can stay in the main house or you can have the guesthouse, your choice. You can drive the SUV while you're here. I'll use the pickup. Also, if you need a place to propose to her either with or without friends or family, you can do it here at home."

"Thanks, Dad. I'll let you know. Listen, I've got to hustle to ensure I get to JFK in time. I'll keep you advised."

"Please do. Be safe, and I look forward to seeing you, son."

"Thanks, Dad. I love you. Bye."

Michael's telephone call had reminded Richard he had promised to call Janet Collins. He assumed their conversation would be fairly short. He wanted to keep his promise before Michael and Shura came to Tucson. He picked up his cell phone and dialed her number.

"Hello, this is Janet."

"Hello, Janet. This is Richard Valencia. I didn't forget about you, but I just received a call from my son in New York. He and his fiancée will be returning to Tucson in a few days. I haven't seen him in over a year, and I don't how long it's been since I saw her. How about if we set a meeting up sooner than later and I'll try to answer any questions you may have? I hope you realize that it's still a work in progress."

"Oh, I do. That's why I can't wait for you to finish. But even if you never get a chance to do so, your draft has already given me a different perspective on life. I don't want to interfere with you and your son and his fiancée. Listen, would tomorrow about seven thirty be OK with you and Jane?"

"Yes. I haven't called her yet, of course, but she indicated she was very much interested in meeting you and speaking with you."

"Good. You caught me on my break. I work from 7:00 a.m. to 7:00 p.m. I get off work tomorrow evening at that time. There is a coffee shop and restaurant very close to the hospital on Speedway just off Mountain Avenue. It's usually very quiet at that time. It's called the Mountain View Cafe. It's popular with the college kids and faculty and the hospital staff. At that time in the evening, it will be pretty quiet. Is that OK?"

"Yes. I'll call Jane, and we'll be there. I look forward to meeting you and talking with you. See you then."

"Thanks, Richard. Goodbye."

Richard dialed Rebecca's home number.

"Hello, this is Rebecca," the voice on the other end answered.

Richard thought he heard a worried thread in Rebecca's voice.

"Hello, Rebecca. This is Richard. How are you and the family?"

"Hunter, William, and I are well. Thanks. I'm concerned about Mother. She had a routine checkup a few days ago, and the results of her blood test apparently caused her oncologist some concern because he asked her to come in the next day after the test results were confirmed. According to him, Mother's cancer may no longer be in remission. He wants to admit her for overnight observation and more tests."

"I am truly sorry to hear that. I will pray for her. She seemed to be doing so well."

"Better than she has in a long time. I have to tell you, Richard, a lot of that has to do with you. You have been wonderful to her. Hold on a second. I believe she's coming down the stairs.

"Mother, it's Richard on the phone. He wants to speak with you."

"Hello, Richard. How nice of you to call. I suppose my daughter blabbed about me. Did she?"

"She told me that your latest test apparently caused your oncologist some concern. Hopefully, it's just a minor glitch and you'll be back to normal soon."

"That would be wonderful. However, I'm a big girl now and have done some research on my cancer. I remain hopeful but realistic. I do, however, put my faith into God's hands. Was there something you wanted to tell me?"

"I called Janet Collins. Just before I did, I received a call from Michael in New York. He is waiting for Shura's flight to arrive from Israel. As soon as she clears customs, he will take her back to the hotel. They are planning to spend a few days together then fly to Tucson for a few more days before traveling to Mexico City to announce their engagement to her family and friends. I wanted us to keep our promise with Janet before the two of them arrived in Tucson so I could devote my attention to them.

"Janet is a nurse and is working from seven in the morning until seven at night. She asked if we could meet her at a coffee shop and restaurant near the hospital close to the university campus. I told I would and that I would call you as soon as I hung up so we could meet her together."

"I'm sorry I'll not be able to go. I was very much looking forward to meeting her and talking with her. I am especially interested in her 'epiphany' she spoke to us about. You go, Richard. There will always be an opportunity for another conversation when I'm through with the hospital. I agree that you should meet her tomorrow so you can be free to devote your time to Michael and Shura."

"Rebecca said you will be there overnight for observation. Is it OK if I call you the day after and perhaps come to see you?"

"Of course. You're always welcome. That's very kind of you. I am a little tired tonight, Richard. I'll say goodbye for now. I'll be interested in hearing about your meeting when I see you. Adios."

"Adios, Jane. I'll pray for you."

Richard set the phone on the table and stood quietly, lost in thought for several minutes. He had a sense of foreboding about Jane. The last time he had seen her, she looked wan. He hadn't really noticed previously, but now he realized that she appeared to have lost some weight. Her clothes not only normally became her but would also make her thinness appear to be less so. He remembered their night together. She was thin but not so much that it appeared to him to be wearisome. He was becoming very fond of Jane. It was not yet quite seven years, Michael had reminded him, since Rachel passed. He had lost two women he loved. What would it be like to lose another? He didn't want to find out, but he knew he couldn't shove it to the back of his mind. He very seldom drank more than an occasional beer or glass of wine with dinner. He walked over to the bar in the living room and poured himself three fingers of Kentucky bourbon.

He had arrived at the Mountain View coffee shop and restaurant at seven twenty. Parking wasn't a problem at this time of night, but he thought that he would hate to try to find street parking during the day, competing with forty-thousand-some students. He didn't order anything when the waitress asked, telling her he would wait for the lady he was expecting. At seven thirty, he received a text on his cell:

I'm running about fifteen minutes late. More paperwork than anticipated. Be there in fifteen minutes; promise. Janet

A little after seven forty-five, he saw a woman in a nurse's scrubs walk into the shop. She stood there for a second, looking around, and then saw him. He waved at her, and she approached his table. She appeared to be about forty-five years or so with thick chestnut brown hair, and when she drew closer, he was struck by her beauty, especially her eyes.

He stood as she approached and offered her his hand.

"Richard Valencia?" she asked.

"Yes. Have a seat. I'm going to order myself a glass of ice tea. Since you just completed a twelve-hour shift, I assume you are probably hungry. What can I order for you, or would you rather wait for the menu? The waitress is on her way."

"I'll also have a glass of ice tea. I am a little hungry. I'm familiar with the menu since I come in here so often. I'm going to have a plate of their chicken fettucine Alfredo with garlic bread. Have you already eaten?"

"Yes, a couple of hours ago."

"Jane couldn't come? I'm sorry. I was looking forward to meeting her. I did a little research on the Internet after we spoke and was impressed by her work and reputation."

"Jane is dealing with some medical issues right now. She's spending tomorrow and tomorrow night in your hospital for observation and some tests. Hopefully, they will be quickly resolved. She did say she was sorry to miss meeting you and hoped she would have another opportunity."

After they were served, Janet began to speak.

"Richard, I mentioned during our last phone conversation that your work had given me a new perspective on life. I understand your insistence that none of the thesis you are compiling is your work but that of others, which you are arranging in a format that can bring some clarity into what I find to be an almost impossible quest, the origin of religion. However, it is your presentation, the way you explain things, at least so far in the draft that I've read, that makes it so special to me.

"I don't know who said that 'life is a journey, not a destination,' but it certainly has application for me. I briefly told you my background of how I arrived, fairly late in life but better late than never, to where I am now. Before becoming a nurse, I was pretty sure that I had made the right decision in becoming an atheist. A lot of religion is superstition and myth. Religion is also the source of much evil and hate in the world even if it also does a lot of good. One of the references you cite in your work is that of Dr. Rupert Sheldrake's book *Morphic Resonance*.[19] I work with many very sick and dying patients. I have personally witnessed the power of prayer and faith into which these patients and their loved ones place their hopes. Maybe it is possible that a fatherly creator in heaven intercedes at the behest of prayer and either cures sickness or makes it more bearable, but I have never been able to accept that. However, Sheldrake gives what I consider a viable hypothesis for this so-called miracle to work, and it seems as if it is basic provable science.

"What really struck me as if a bolt of lightning out of the blue was your discussion about revealed religion. I think you once believed that the myths of religion that speak to the Almighty interceding in human affairs to the benefit of the faithful are mostly wishful thinking. But Velikovsky's genius was in providing a natural cause for much of what is believed as divine intervention.

"I have to tell you that during my undergraduate years, I took an elective course in Russian literature. I enjoyed it immensely because the authors I read were masters of their genre and wrote about the life and times in history they experienced. But there was one work in particular that struck an emotional response in me and gave me a better sense of understanding the religious fervor that my parents and members of their church experienced. When we studied the works of the Russian poet Pushkin, I read his poem *The Prophet*, and it was as if I experienced myself the divine revelation from the Almighty by an archangel. That poem awakened the sense of terror and foreboding I felt as a young girl during religious services and discussions with our pastor. I don't know if it could be called a post-traumatic flashback to my youth, but it literally set a milestone in my life that I cannot forget.

---

[19] Rupert Sheldrake, *Morphic Resonance: The Nature of Formative Causation* (Rochester, Vermont: Park Street Press, 2009).

"I remember sitting in a cold and darkened church during a service when the pastor, as part of his sermon, spoke about Isaiah's vision of God in the temple. He spoke of six-winged seraphs in attendance calling to one another, saying, 'Holy, holy is the Lord of hosts, the whole earth is full of his glory.' Isaiah was struck like the prophet in Pushkin's poem. He trembled in fear as the very foundations of the temple shook and the room was filled with smoke. He cried out in desperation that he was lost because he was a sinner, a man of unclean lips, yet he had seen the King, the Lord of Hosts. I recall the preacher pausing before continuing. The congregation was silent, no one coughed, there were no children crying. They, like me, were transfixed by his words, which he spoke in a booming voice. Then he went on to describe how one of the seraphs took a burning coal with a pair of tongs and touched Isaiah's mouth with it, saying to the prophet that he was now cleansed of sin. Then Isaiah heard the voice of the Lord, asking, 'Whom shall I send, and who will go for us?' The preacher paused again and finished by telling us that Isaiah responded, saying, 'Here am I. Send me!'[20]

"When I read the draft of your book, I experienced something similar to the flashback to a dark time in my life. How am I doing so far? Am I basically on track with your work?"

"Yes, basically, but we can discuss the subtleties later. By the way, I believe it was Emerson, Ralph Waldo Emerson, who said that life is a journey."

"Thanks. I'll remember that. Whoever said it, it is entirely correct. Now let me explain why I said your work about revealed religion was an epiphany for me. Ancient humans witnessed the events in the solar system, which was reconfiguration after the binary star system was captured. They attributed these events to those of the gods originally but, after monotheism held sway, to God. From the origins of religion from an astral basis, man has developed, like you state, a complex and sophisticated theology.

---

[20] Isaiah 6:1–8, New Revised Standard Version (NRSV).

However, the basics remain. Without humans, there would be no religion on earth as you've stated. But that doesn't negate the possibility that God, whether He is a person or the universe itself, is not revealing Himself or Itself to man. What struck me is that everyone's definition of God includes the attribute of omniscience or of all knowing. We humans, as you point out, can only conceive of the ability of knowing, including omniscience, as resulting from a mind or something akin to a mind. And if God is all powerful, omnipotent, then He can reveal Himself or anything else He desires to mankind or any other conscious being.

"I have held abandoned and very sick children in my arms. Sometimes a loving, caring touch will do wonders for them, and I have seen not only sick children but adults as well respond to caring human touch. As you quote in your work, touch is but one method of human transference. I believe that there is significant evidence to show that human transference through touch can help heal the sick. I also believe that is where the positive effects of prayer come in. It is part of human transference but of a nonphysical source, perhaps energy in some form from one person or persons to another."

She paused, finished eating, and then placed her plate and silverware to the side of the table. She hadn't touched the garlic bread. He saw that she was animated; her deep blue eyes seemed to radiate wonder and joy at what she was telling him.

"Richard, if you knew me as my family and friends know me, you would be greatly surprised by my words tonight. I have been a true and dedicated nonbeliever if that even makes any sense. But reading your work, and that of others cited in your thesis, has opened new doors for me. Actually, I believe my future is greatly more optimistic about life than it was before Dr. Glickman gave me your draft. I hope we can have further discussions. There is so much more I want to learn. I even reread the creation account in Genesis with a new perspective and understanding. The words are even more beautiful to me now than before. Promise me we will have more discussions like this."

"I'll try. I find you a very fascinating and interesting woman. I won't insult your intelligence by telling you that you are beautiful as well as intellectual."

"I think you just did, but believe me, I take it as a compliment."

Neither said anything for a minute or so, but it was not an awkward silence. It seemed as if each was trying to capture their conversation.

"May I ask you a favor?" she asked, looking intently at him.

"Yes, of course. What can I do?"

"Earlier on my break, right before you called, I attempted to start my car because I was going to make a trip to the local convenience store to get some slushies for myself and two other nurses. Unfortunately, I couldn't start my car. I think the battery is dead. I called a friend of mine who is a mechanic, and he promised he would check it out tomorrow morning. He will pick up the key from me then see if it's the battery or something worse, and he promised to have it ready for me tomorrow evening when I get off work. I was going to catch a taxi home, but I was wondering if you could drop me off. It's not too far from here, but I don't feel comfortable walking alone at night or catching the bus, and sometimes the taxi takes a long time in arriving."

"I would be happy to. When would you like to leave?"

"Now. We've been talking for almost an hour already. I didn't mean to keep you so long, but it seemed right to talk with you."

He drove her to the University Shadows apartment complex. It was gated, and she activated the gate with a remote device that reminded Richard of his garage door opener. He walked her to the door of the apartment. The complex was attractive, well landscaped with sufficient lighting along the pathways to ensure safe, well-lit passage.

She unlocked the door and then said, "Please come in for a while. I'll make you a glass of ice tea and a snack if you want. I won't keep you long."

Richard didn't answer immediately. It was against his better judgment. *Don't do this, Richard,* he thought. *There is significant risk if you do.* Then he thought, *Richard, now is not the time to hesitate. Being with her is strongly appealing.* After she placed his glass of tea on the table next to where he sat, she sat next to him on the edge so she could easily face him.

"There is something I have yet to tell you about my epiphany, Richard. I want to tell you now. Please listen."

"I will."

He looked into her eyes and was captivated by the way she looked at him.

"I mentioned my phone call to you with Jane present that I had informed my parents that I was a lesbian."

Richard began to say that it was not important to him, but she put a finger to his lips to silence him.

"Margaret and I had a relationship for three years. We considered marriage once same-sex marriage became legal in California but decided against it. We were already beginning to have differences. We were not different from any other couple. Maintaining a relationship requires work and constant attention to your partner. I was the one that began to drift away primarily because once I decided I wanted to become a nurse and work in Africa, I devoted almost all my energy to achieve that goal. I realize that I failed her, and I deeply regret it to this day. We drifted apart until she informed me that she had found someone else with whom she would be happier. In a way, I was sad but somewhat relieved to be able to pursue my goal with all my ability.

"Richard, for the first time in my life, tonight when I saw you, a totally unfamiliar emotion almost overwhelmed me. It has been many, many years since I've been attracted to a man, let alone desired to have a relationship with one. Tonight when

I saw you, I felt an overwhelming need to be with you, to have you hold me. I am not foolish enough to believe that you and I could have a relationship. Richard, I want you. I want to be part of your life if only briefly. Please come lie with me."

He could only remember certain aspects of what happened that night. She placed her arms around his neck and kissed him with a passion that quickly ignited his and which surged through his body with an irresistible force. She dropped her arms and, while still standing close to him, removed her clothes. Richard could not help himself as his eyes caressed her body from her face to her feet several times. He did not resist as she pulled his shirt from his trousers and removed it, throwing it on the floor beside them. She unbuckled his belt and pulled his pants down to his shoes, which he quickly removed and cast aside on the carpet with the pants. She slowly removed his undershorts, exposing his hardened and throbbing desire for her. Richard was startled as she gently led him to the bed and into her arms. He did not resist as she rolled him over and mounted him. She did not move but tenderly kissed his forehead, his nose, his chin, and then his lips. He wanted to remain locked in her embrace for as long as possible. He did not want the moment to end.

"Richard," she softly whispered, "I need to do this. I know you will understand."

He did. She was passionate in a gentle, loving way.

Afterward, they lay silent. He thought of Cathy, he thought of Rachel, he thought of Naomi, he thought of Jane.

When he didn't speak, she did. "It is all right. I can understand what you are probably experiencing right now. Call it woman's intuition or whatever. We will both be able to put this into perspective later. Do you want to get up and go home?"

"No."

They remained together through the night until the early hours before dawn. She gently turned aside his attempts to touch her tenderly but held him closely. She turned her back to him, placed his arms around her, and softly began to sleep. He fell asleep after several minutes of listening to her breathe.

The smell of coffee and bacon and eggs awakened him. He looked at the clock on the nightstand. It was 6:00 a.m. He remembered that she had to be at work at 7:00 a.m. He quickly dressed and entered the kitchen.

"Good morning, Richard," she said. "Have a seat. I've taken the liberty of making you breakfast because I have to leave shortly to be at work on time. Do you mind dropping me off?"

"No. Thanks. I'm famished."

She smiled at him.

"Richard, about last night," she said as she exited the car at the hospital, "I have something more to share with you, something terribly important to me, and I believe you will understand. This is not the time. I will explain it to you later when I don't have to rush off."

"Goodbye," he replied.

Richard drove slowly home, reliving every moment from the time she walked into the restaurant until he had dropped her off at the hospital. What had happened? He was uncertain.

CHAPTER TEN

EPIPHANY

Once back home, Richard showered and shaved. He went to the kitchen and made a pot of coffee. He glanced at the newspaper while he waited for the coffee to brew, but it was only cursory. When the coffee was ready, he poured himself a mug and then went into the living room and sat in the recliner, sipped his coffee, and then placed it on the table next to the chair.

What just happened? I feel as though my encounter with Janet held a deeper meaning that I have yet to comprehend. What was it?

She had come to him because she had read the draft of his work, the origin of religion. She believed, as many atheists do, that once life ends here on earth, that is the end. Just as they have no memory of existence prior to birth, so they expect to have no consciousness after death. But religious faith is the spoiler. Whatever else religious faith brings to the believer, it is hope, hope for something beyond death. That entails having a reason to live for something more significant than just the maintenance and worldly enjoyment of life. She had mentioned that her religious upbringing essentially taught that she was born sinful and in need of God's grace for salvation. She was unworthy of life beyond death unless she committed herself to certain beliefs and actions. Some people who professed such faith held serious doubts; some did not believe.

Janet's epiphany, as he understood it, was that her new knowledge helped her realize that there were physical manifestations of the universe surrounding mankind that could be explained by physical science ever better as man learned more. But a greater understanding is that man's increasing learning of his universe is but one aspect of revelation. The events of the universe do not require man's awareness of them to exist, only to appreciate and marvel at its nature and his part in it. The universe reveals itself to humans as they continue to learn more about it. That revelation can be thought by a scientist to be the result of greater understanding through learning, experience, and experiment. But it can also be thought of by others as a heavenly, loving father directly revealing himself to them through religious channels or, as some mystics believe, through meditation. Those believers don't have to understand, nor do they desire to understand what they believe to be the will of a loving and caring Creator. Why question God's motives? Our limited human capability makes us forever unable to fully understand the Almighty. Many seek it through the written word or through priests, shamans, or rabbis or through experience with the spiritual nature of the universe.

He would have time to talk with her more thoroughly in the future. He believed he knew the almost overwhelming force that attracted each to the other; it was a force greater than anything else the universe has expressed itself to mankind: love. Love is a universal force that gives humans a meaning for life, a meaning beyond mere existence. A Darwinian evolutionist would state that love is merely a survival mechanism to ensure that the race survives. But to what end is survival? He realized that he could come to love Janet because love would bind their souls together in their search for truth. If not truth, then it was a basic understanding as far as their limited ability of being human would allow. Religious experience through love and sex—a cynic would question such a belief as rationalization. Richard knew better. Richard labored to compile how ancient man came to understand and explain the physical manifestations of creation and God's revelation. The identity of the cause of this revelation took essentially the same expression but with different beliefs with different names. Some of those names included Yahweh and his consort—Asherah, El, Elohim, Aten, Ra, Saturn, Cronus, Vishnu, Kukulkan, Quetzalcoatl, and the electromagnetic force.

Jane! How could he have forgotten? Richard put his thoughts away and called the hospital to determine which room Jane was in and when visiting hours were.

"She's in room 3562. Visiting hours are between eight o'clock in the morning and eight o'clock in the evening. She is scheduled for several events today, so the best time to visit would either be during the noon hour or after three in the afternoon," the operator informed him.

Richard arrived at the hospital at three thirty and took the elevator to the fifth floor, quickly finding Jane's room. He knocked softly on the doorframe. She was alone.

"Come in, Richard. It's so good to see you." She smiled.

"You're looking good today, Jane. How do you feel?"

He watched the smile leave her face as she paused before she spoke.

"Tired, Richard. I feel very tired today. I have learned that my cancer has returned with a vengeance and has already spread to my kidneys, spleen, and liver. Both my oncologist and Rebecca are trying to be optimistic, but I'm afraid that after all we've done, after all I've been through, the cancer is winning. I'm tired, but thank God, they've given me enough pain medication to keep it at a manageable level."

Richard repositioned a chair from the wall to the side of her bed, sat, and took her hand in his.

"It's not necessary, Richard. You don't have to say anything. I am determined to accept my fate and to ask them simply to mitigate my pain. My time is coming. I can feel it. I am not afraid. I believe strongly in Jesus and have prayed to Him my entire life. I look forward to being with Him. Don't look so sad, please. I don't want you to be sad."

"I won't, Jane. When is Rebecca returning? I would like to speak with her."

"She said she would be here later this evening, probably about seven o'clock. She has to pick William up from baseball practice. He's quite an athlete. He plays second base and has a batting average of over three hundred! I'm so proud of him.

"Oh, I almost forgot to mention it to you. Janet Collins stopped by to see me earlier this morning. That nice bouquet of mums on the table is from her. She said she learned that I was in the hospital from her meeting with you the other night. How did that go?"

"It went well," Richard replied, somewhat uncertain on how to proceed.

"That's good," Jane said. "I really like her. We didn't talk much about anything other than she was concerned for me and told me to have my nurse call her if I ever needed anything. She even told the nurse on the way out. I told her that when I left the hospital, we would get together and speak about her ideas and your work. She was kind enough to tell me she had purchased several copies of my books and has started to read them."

Jane fell silent and didn't speak for several minutes. Richard sat quietly with her hand in his. Her hand felt much frailer than he remembered when he held her while dancing.

"You know, Richard, when I mentioned that we would get together after I leave the hospital, I saw the expression in her eyes change, and she had to turn away briefly because she began to tear up. I told her to please not worry about me. I am in a good place. No one lives forever, and I have been fortunate in my life. I had wonderful parents, a good education, fell in love with a wonderful man, and raised a beautiful daughter with him, and I have a wonderful grandson. I was very fortunate to be able to pursue my passion.

"Maybe it was David who wrote in the fourteenth Psalm that the fool has said in his heart there is no God. Maybe he did, maybe he didn't. I don't believe we will ever know. I believe. Death for me is a door to a new paradise. No matter how much learning I've been able to achieve, my faith still comes down to just that, faith. I hope that you will have that certainty as well. You have both a Christian Catholic and Jewish faith to guide you. It is I who will pray for you, Richard. I hope you find what you are looking for. I'm only sorry I won't be able to read your work when it's finished, but I have no doubt that it will be a worthy effort.

"Richard, thank you for coming. I feel like I need to sleep. Would you ask the nurse to come in when you leave?"

"Yes, Jane. I will keep in touch with Rebecca, and I promise I'll come to see you tomorrow."

"Goodbye, Richard. *Vaya con Dios.*"

"I'll see you tomorrow, Jane."

CHAPTER ELEVEN

FAREWELL

Richard visited Jane every day until she passed on Friday evening at ten o'clock, six days after she had been admitted for testing. Although Janet had called him several times on his cell phone, he did not answer. She left one message saying that she understood what he was going through and she would be there for him when he needed her. All he had to do was to let her know.

Janet was familiar with Jane's condition since she was a nurse at the hospital. Somehow Richard knew that he would not see her when he came to see Jane. He knew she would purposely avoid him to give him space to deal with his sorrow. He didn't know how much Janet knew about his feelings toward Jane. He knew that she frequently visited her bedside from conversations with Rebecca and from the attending nurse or nurse's aides he spoke with. He was certain that they had discussed their close, if brief, relationship and how Rebecca had noticed his effect on her mother.

He had learned from Rebecca when he arrived that she had passed not nearly an hour earlier. She had been heavily sedated as per her living will so that she would pass as pain free and comfortable as possible.

Rebecca promised him she would let him know about funeral arrangements as soon as possible. He softly whispered goodbye to Jane. He left the room but did not go home. He knew Janet was working in the children's ward and was now on a 7:00 p.m. to 7:00 a.m. schedule. He slowly walked toward the children's ward, and when he entered, he asked the nurse at the desk where she might be.

"Janet's in room 2345 with a patient," the nurse told him and motioned to the room toward the end of the hall.

"Thanks. Can I see her?" he asked.

"Yes," she replied, turning to answer the phone.

He walked slowly down the hall, and when he approached the room, he hesitated at the door. He saw Janet sitting in a recliner, holding what appeared to him to be a nine- or ten-year-old child. He could not determine whether she was holding a girl or a boy. It was obvious that she held a special-needs child. From the posture of the child, Richard believed that he or she was suffering from a paralysis muscular condition. Janet, at first, did not notice him, but after a few minutes, she looked at him and smiled.

"Hello, Richard. It's nice of you to come. Come here. I'll introduce you to Michael."

She looked at him with understanding in her eyes as he approached the chair.

"Richard, I am so sorry for your loss. Jason was her nurse on duty, and he called to let me know of her passing earlier. If there is anything I can do, please let me know."

"I will. Who is your patient?"

"This beautiful child is Michael Callendar. He is ten years old, and he was born with Duchenne muscular dystrophy or DMD. Unfortunately, his father left when he was very young. According to his mother, he just could not deal with his son's condition and all that it entails. His mother is a nurse's aide who works the night shift at Tucson Medical Center across town. Michael has been sound asleep for about twenty minutes or so." She gently brushed the boy's thick brown hair on the side of his head as he slept.

"He will sleep for several hours now. He was exhausted from his therapy earlier this evening and had difficulty falling asleep."

She lifted him as she arose from the chair with apparent ease. Richard was struck by her strength. She gently walked with Michael in her arms the few steps to his bed and gently laid him down and covered him with a sheet. She adjusted the bedding to ensure he was as comfortable as she could make him. After several minutes, she turned to Richard.

"Richard, if you need a hug, come."

He came to her, and she placed her arms around him and held him for several minutes in silence. He held her closely but gently. He closed his eyes and felt his need for her suffuse through him. She pulled slowly away and looked at him.

"I know," she said.

She didn't need to explain. He knew.

CHAPTER TWELVE

DANCE

Richard waited in the baggage area while Michael and Shura deplaned off their flight from New York. He watched the live display of disembarking passengers walking toward the stairway to the baggage claim area, where he waited, hoping to see his son and soon-to-be daughter-in-law approach. He was filled with joy and pride as he saw his son and Shura walking toward him on the monitor. Michael had lost weight it seemed to him. He was more slender than when he had last seen him, which made him appear taller than his six feet two inches. He was holding hands with Shura. Richard realized that she was even more beautiful than he had remembered. She was now a fully matured woman and not the college coed he remembered her as.

Shura released Michael's hand and stepped forward to embrace Richard and kiss him on each cheek.

"Mr. Valencia," she greeted, "you look good and fit. It is wonderful to see you again!"

"Michael," he answered, "you are indeed a lucky man to have such a beautiful fiancée. Both of you look great. I am so happy to see you again safe and away from danger. Shura, please call me Richard."

Richard embraced his son and held him firmly for several seconds, thanking God for his safe return.

"Let's get your luggage and leave. Are you hungry?" Richard asked.

"We actually had a fairly good steak with wine on the airplane since we booked the premium class. Everything else was booked for this flight. How about if we just head home, Dad? We can always rustle something up later if we get hungry. I've been in the States for several weeks, but Shura just arrived a few days ago and is still suffering from jet lag."

The conversation was animated during the drive home. Both Michael and Shura marveled at the changes that had occurred in Tucson since they were last here. Once home, Richard helped Michael carry their bags into the guesthouse, for which they had both expressed their preference.

"I enjoyed our few days in New York," Shura said. "But I'm still recovering from the trip. It will be nice to sleep in as long as we want and not have to worry about disturbing you, Richard."

"You won't disturb me. I can't tell you how excited I am to have you here again. But you two lovebirds will naturally prefer to be alone. I understand," Richard said.

"How about if we shower and change and then we'll join you in the house? I will have a cold beer, and Shura can choose whatever she wants. Then tomorrow we throw some steaks on the grill," Michael replied.

"Great. Take your time. I'll make myself a quick sandwich and a glass of tea and watch the evening news until you two are ready."

Richard was not only joyous to see his son but relieved as well. Although he had flown in combat, it had been a long time ago when he was an aircrewman in the navy's Super Hornet. Ground combat was much more difficult and dangerous. He could only imagine what Michael and Shura had experienced. He decided not to ask questions but to let them tell him what they wanted him to know at their own pace. The last thing he desired was to be perceived as nosy or meddling into their affairs.

He thought of the two women most recently in his life, Jane and Janet. Although he knew that Jane had been fighting her cancer for years, she seemed so positive and optimistic about her chance of recovery that even when he noticed she appeared to be increasingly thin and tired, he did not expect what to him was her rapid and unexpected death. In one of their many conversations about his work, she had told him that she thought perhaps one motivation that drove him was to better understand how religion answers mankind's eternal question about death and what lies beyond it. She was correct as she normally was in matters of religion and spirituality. What about Janet? She was an avowed atheist. Something in his effort to better understand the origin of religion seemed to have awakened her to a wider perspective than that of the atheist, an epiphany he remembered as she had described it.

The next week was joyous and meaningful to Richard. The day after Michael and Shura arrived was spent at home resting and talking. Michael had insisted on barbecuing so that his dad could just sit back and relax, not realizing how much Richard wanted to do things for his son and fiancée. But he let them take the lead. In the evening over wine, they sat in the living room and talked about whatever came to their mind. When Richard mentioned that Michael had written in one of his letters that he would formally propose to Shura in Tucson, he did so.

Michael knelt on one knee and produced a beautiful diamond ring from his pocket and proposed. "Shura, I love you with all my heart and soul and want to spend the rest of my life with you. Will you marry me?"

Shura reached down to him, taking him by the hands and lifting her to him. She placed her hands over his shoulder as she had done in that faraway embattled land when he had first asked her.

"Yes, I will, Michael. Forever, I will love and cherish you forever."

Shura beamed with joy when Michael placed a beautiful round-cut diamond on her finger.

"I know you don't remember, but when we were discussing your friend Barbara's engagement ring, you said that it was a beautiful marquise cut, but if you ever got engaged, you would hope for a round cut. I can see why. The jeweler told me that the round-cut diamond will amplify the sparkle and brightness the most. I immediately knew that it fits your personality. Shura, you also amplify the brightness of your life with a luster that will forever sparkle in my memory."

"Michael, Barbara got engaged over five years ago! How did you remember?"

"Because, Shura, I have been in love with you for much longer than five years, and I hoped this day would come. You've just made me a happy man by saying yes, you'll marry me."

Shura came to Richard and held her hand up so he could more closely see the ring.

"Look, Dad, how beautiful it is. I am so happy that you are here to share this moment with us. You will soon be my father-in-law, but I will forever call you Dad from this moment on."

Richard could only embrace her close to him. He felt tears in his eyes and could not speak, overcome with emotion as he was.

When they released each other, Shura saw the tears in his eyes and kissed him on the cheek.

"I am so glad you approve," she said.

The next two days were a busy time for the newly engaged couple. The following afternoon, they had seven friends over for a barbecue and reunion. Four of the seven had made their careers away from Tucson and happened to be visiting. The other three lived in Tucson, where they made their careers. One was an attractive young lady by the name of Juanita Marques.

Richard learned more about both Juanita and Shura when the three of them engaged in conversation while Michael was attending to the steaks on the grill.

"Dad, Juanita and I were good friends when we were students at the university. We met when she was majoring in Mexican American studies and I was working toward a minor in Judaic studies. At that time, the administrative offices were located on the same floor of the social sciences building. We eventually became good friends. Juanita was then a member of a club called Los Universitarios, and since I was from Mexico and spoke Spanish as a first language, I was readily accepted into the club. I eventually became a member.

"It was during that time when Juanita, who was also working toward a degree in education, was volunteering with a local *folkórico* group of middle and high school students. Although she was a volunteer, she also received credits in her education major for working with young students. My mother, who is as proud of her Mexican heritage as that of her Jewish, had enrolled me in a local *folkórico* club when I was in middle school, and I became good enough to participate in several concerts patterned after the world-famous Ballet Folkórico de Mexico. At her invitation and that of the group's leader, Mrs. Duran, I too volunteered as an instructor and was actually able to participate in several concerts with the group throughout Arizona, California, and Nevada."

"We even were invited to perform in a concert at the John F. Kennedy Center for the Performing Arts in Washington," Juanita said. "Shura is much too modest. She is a gifted *folklórico* performer, not only as a dancer but also as a singer. You should hear her belt out her rendition of Jalisco if you ever get a chance, Mr. Valencia."

"I would love to. Shura, are you game?" Richard smiled.

"It's been too long, Dad, and too much water has passed under the bridge. I'm not even sure I can carry a tune."

"Don't be so modest, Shura!" Juanita replied. "Listen, our club is scheduled to present a concert at the Jewish Community Center for the Horowitz Assisted Living facility this Sunday afternoon. Why don't you join us? We have a two-hour practice each day until then. I'm sure it wouldn't take you long to get your groove back."

"I accept!" Shura laughed as she replied. "I would love to dance joyfully again. I would love to dance for my fiancé to show him how happy he has made me. And for my dad who is happy for the two of us. Mexican folk dancing can be of many moods, but it is at its best when it celebrates joy, love, and living. Thank you, Juanita, for thinking of me this way. Do you think there will be a costume available that will fit me?"

"Honey, with your figure, you could easily pass as one of the high school girls in the entourage. Are you kidding? I'm not admitting that I'm envious of your girlish looks, but whatever you've done since graduation has kept you fit and trim."

The smile disappeared off Shura's face at her friend's innocent remark. "Juanita, someday when we are both mothers, I will tell you about some of my years since graduation. But here and now, I will only live in my joy and happiness. You have my commitment to practice hard. I won't stick out like a sore thumb. Dad, do you think you will be able to attend?"

"I wouldn't miss it for the world. I want to be there to share Michael's experience when he sees his fiancée dancing for him."

The remainder of the day was enjoyable for Richard. He basked in the friendship and celebration of his son and Shura's happy reunion with their friends. In the evening, when everyone had departed and Michael and Shura were in the guesthouse, he wondered, *Should I invite Janet to come with me? Is it too soon? What would Michael and Shura think? Knowing them as I do, they would be happy for me to see me with a companion if even for just an evening.* He decided he would ask her.

"I would love to come, Richard. Thank you for asking. I am looking forward to meeting your son and his fiancée. I am scheduled to work Sunday but will have no trouble getting Vera to work for me. I worked for her on a Sunday during my regular day off so she could celebrate her son's First Communion, and she had been grateful to me ever since. What time should I be ready?"

"The concert starts at two, but Shura will have to be there no later than one to prepare for it. Michael will be taking her in the SUV. You'll get to ride in my good old Ford pickup. I hope you don't mind."

"Not at all. I love trucks. I was thinking of trading my Hyundai in for one, but then when would I ever use it? I'm not a hunter or fisherman. I just fancy myself driving around in boots, jeans, and a ten-gallon hat."

Richard laughed. "Great. I'll pick you up a little after one. I'll see you then."

The Jewish Community Center was a large complex on the near north side of Tucson with a large fully equipped playground, tennis courts, and a garden memorial for those who had perished in the Holocaust. Richard knew from previous experience that the complex included a gym with two hardwood basketball courts, an indoor pool, a well-equipped weight room, several meeting rooms, and a large theater with a stage with excellent acoustics. When they arrived, the parking lot was half filled. He noticed a white-painted bus with the words "Horowitz Assisted Living" painted on the side in black letters.

Michael greeted them as they entered the theater. He introduced him to Janet.

"It is nice to meet you, Janet," Michael said.

"The pleasure is mine, Michael," she replied. "Richard has not spoken of you at length, but when he mentions you, it is obvious that he is very proud of you and loves you a great deal."

"Thank you, Janet. Dad, as family, we have reserved seats in the center section near the front. Our names are marked on a card on the seats. I promised Shura that I would come back stage to be with her as soon as you arrived. I'll join you before the performance starts."

"Take your time, Michael. I promise I won't get lost." Richard smiled at his son. "Listen, when you get a chance, I want to introduce you to Nathan Phillips. I see him over there. He is the mayor of Tucson and also a member of our University Synagogue."

"I'd love to. I'll be back before the performance begins," Michael replied as he walked toward the stage.

"I know Mayor Phillips," Janet said. "He is good friends with Aaron Silver. You do remember who Aaron Silver is?"

"I do. You said he is a neurosurgeon at the university hospital and also president of your Arizona Atheists Association. Am I correct?"

"Yes! Good! He and Mayor Phillips are good friends. It seems as if they've known each other since childhood and even attended the same Hebrew school together. After college, the mayor went to law school, and Aaron went to medical school. Somewhere along the line, Aaron became a devoted atheist, and as far as I know, the mayor is still an observant Jew."

"He is, Janet. He is a member of a Reformed congregation, University Synagogue, which my family has been members of for years. I don't know him as a friend, but we are on a first-name basis having attended several functions together over the years, most often when Rachel was alive."

Nathan noticed the two of them and walked toward them, greeting them with a smile.

"Richard, Janet, how good to see you. I am looking forward to seeing this young group perform again. I have seen them several times at other assisted-living facilities around town, and they are a talented group of musicians and dancers. Are you both fans of Mexican folk music?"

"Actually, Nathan, my son's new fiancée is performing. She was born in Mexico City and actually performed *folklórico* as a middle school and high school student. She recently met a college friend who works with this group and was invited to perform. Both Michael and I are eagerly looking forward to seeing her do so."

"I would be too, Richard. How is Aaron, Janet? Is he behaving himself?" Nathan asked.

"Yes, he and his wife made a quick trip to Phoenix this weekend to attend a meeting."

"Don't tell me it was an AAA meeting." Turning to Richard, Nathan said, "Arizona Association of Atheists, Richard. Aaron does not have a drinking problem. It's something that some people confuse."

"I know." Richard laughed as he answered. "Janet here is also a member."

"Are you in a midlife crisis?" Nathan asked Richard, smiling. "I'm not serious, Richard. Do you still attend services?"

"You have nothing to worry about, Mr. Mayor," Richard replied. "I do, although I will admit not nearly as often since Rachel passed. I will be attending next Friday with Michael and his fiancée, Shura, to say Kaddish for Rachel. It's something they both asked to do."

"That's wonderful. Dinah and I will be there as well."

"I would love to attend with you Richard, if it's possible," Janet asked.

"It is not only possible, but we would also love to have you, Janet," Nathan replied. "I hope you do. Listen, I believe people are moving to their seats because we are only minutes away from the performance. It's been very enjoyable talking with both of you. I hope to see you both next Friday. Richard, be sure to give Michael and Shura my congratulations and best wishes if I don't get a chance to meet them after the performance. I actually have to leave a little before its scheduled ending for another commitment across town."

After they were seated, Janet said, "Richard, I hope I'm not rude. When I said I would like to attend services with you, it was because I would like to see a Jewish service. I've never attended one. Now, however, I realized that Rachel is your deceased wife, and I believe Kaddish is a prayer for the dead. It may not be appropriate for me to attend this service with you and your son and his fiancée. Perhaps I should attend services with you another time."

"Let me think this through, Janet. I am not an Orthodox Jew, but I do try to honor and respect Halacha or Jewish religious law. I do know, mostly through my deceased wife's teaching, that Kaddish is now permitted to be said by women since essentially the thirteenth century. She would also sometimes quote a Rabbi by the name of Hillel: 'That which is hateful unto you do not do to your neighbor. This is the whole of the Torah, the rest is commentary. Go forth and study.' To me, the underlying thought is of goodwill. If it is your intention to honor and respect a person by attending a service in which Kaddish will be said, then it is acceptable. At least it is to me. Also, the reason Michael and Shura wish to attend is to ensure that there will be a minyan or enough male members who completed Bar Mitzvah to guarantee a quorum for prayer, including the Kaddish. Most others will not be saying Kaddish for Rachel. So yes, please attend services with us. We would be honored that you honor and respect Rachel. Most people there won't even know that you're not Jewish. Only the mayor and his wife will know that you're an atheist, but their goodwill and hospitality will be evident."

She grasped his hand. "Richard, you are a remarkable man. I so want to get to know you better, and I want to discuss with you your work and religion. I know this is not the time or place, but I hope we will see more of each other."

"We will," he replied as he turned his head to greet Michael, who was taking his seat next to him.

"I am looking forward to this," Michael said. "She is happy and joyous and filled with laughter. It has been a long, long journey from Iraq."

The lights were dimmed, and a hush fell over the audience as two women climbed the steps to the stage and positioned themselves behind the lectern. Michael recognized Juanita Marques. She was accompanied by an attractive woman who obviously was an official of the center as she wore a lanyard with a tag of some sort.

"Ladies and gentlemen, please welcome Ms. Juanita Marques, who is the owner and head instructor of Folkórico Tucson. Folkórico Tucson is a club of middle school and high school students who learn the folk dances and songs of Mexico as part of their general education. They are a talented group of young people who volunteer their talents to entertain many diverse groups of people, including elderly residents of nursing homes and assisted-living facilities. They have performed through the southwest and in Washington DC as well as in Mexico. Last year, they won first place in a *folklórico* competition, which included not only groups from Tucson but also California, Nevada, Texas, New Mexico, and Mexico. Ms. Marques is also a principal at Raymond Wilson Middle School and is active in many local civic organizations. Please welcome Ms. Juanita Marques."

The audience applauded as Juanita began to speak.

"Thank you, Mrs. Golden. Thank you for your kind words, your hospitality, and your invitation to perform here at the Jewish Community Center for the Horowitz Assisted Living Facility. Our young people are eager to display their artistic achievements in the folk music, dance, and songs of Mexico. Many of our students continue their performance as they go on to higher education or into their careers. I would like to announce a special treat for you tonight. A dear friend with whom I attended university has recently returned to Tucson with her fiancé to visit her soon-to-be father-in-law. She was born and raised in Mexico City, where she learned *folklórico* dancing as a middle school student. She also volunteered in instructing middle and high school students while she attended the university. She has since graduated, of course, and has pursued a career overseas. I will introduce you to her after the performance. She was a little concerned because it had been several years since she actually danced *folklórico*. However, I told her she needn't worry because she is a gifted performer as you will see tonight. Let's begin with Mariachi Alegre of Folkórico Tucson!"

The curtain rose and revealed a mariachi band composed of young men and women students dressed in traditional attire. The audience applauded and cheered as they began a rousing rendition of "Guadalajara." After several minutes, a line of dancers entered the stage. The male students were dressed in the traditional vaquero costume of Jalisco with their wide-brimmed sombreros and black leather boots. The female students were striking in their wide flowing skirts of different colors and embroidered design and their white embroidered blouses and white high heel boots.

Richard and Michael both immediately recognized Shura. She was striking in her beauty. Like the other women, she held her head back in the proud but flirtatious manner so recognizable in *folklórico* dancing. She had certainly not lost her ability to perform as she danced with carefree joy to the music. Richard glanced at the audience and then at Janet. Both were spellbound by the performance. He then glanced at his son, who gazed intensely at his fiancée. He noticed tears in his eyes. He looked again at Shura, who also gazed at Michael as she tossed her head and moved her feet with high-stepping energy and enthusiasm. He could only wonder at this woman whom his son revealed had experienced hard and terrible combat in Iraq with a ruthless and cruel enemy driven by religious fanaticism. That she could dance for her beloved with so much joy and eloquence was truly remarkable.

After the first number was completed, the women and men, eight to each group, danced to opposite ends of the stage. There was a brief pause, and then Mariachi Alegre again broke into spirited music. The men danced across the stage with both hands clasped behind their backs, forming a line. Each dancer moved his feet in unison to the music, pirouetting and stomping their feet on the stage. They twirled again in unison and then danced backward to their side of the stage. The women then danced across the stage, stepping and pirouetting with their colorful skirts in their hands, their heads held high, glancing over their shoulders as they turned. The women formed a line in the middle of the stage, dancing in place, while the men again danced in a line, feet tapping vigorously against the stage. They formed a line in front of the women, who then danced to their side. Shura was paired with a tall, athletic young man. Now formed into couples, each man and woman locked arms and danced in a circle. The men grasped their wide-brimmed sombreros and swept them off their head, holding them waist high. The couples separated slightly, providing room for the men to throw their sombreros on the stage between them and their partner. At this point, the almost universally recognized rhythm of the Mexican hat dance reverberated across the audience, which burst into applause.

The lady seated next to Richard turned to him and said, "I don't know who that beautiful girl in the center is, but her partner is Miguel Orozco. He is an All-American first baseman on the university's baseball team who helped them win the national championship at the college world series last year. I had no idea he could dance so beautifully."

Richard could not help but smile at the woman and whispered with a great deal of pride, "That beautiful girl he is dancing with will soon be my son's bride!"

The lady bent over and looked across Richard and Janet to Michael, who was obviously engrossed in the performance and wasn't aware of the discussion between his father and the lady.

She put her hand to her face and whispered, "He's your son?"

"He is," Richard replied.

"Is she the one Ms. Marques referred to at the introduction?"

"I believe so."

"You are a lucky man." She smiled and turned her attention to the performance.

"Thank you," Richard replied and smiled at Janet, who had listened to the brief exchange.

When Richard again looked at the stage, he noticed that Shura and her partner, whose name he now knew, Miguel, were alone, separated from the other dancers, who, in couples, stood behind them toward the rear of the stage in front of the mariachi band. He would later learn from Juanita that, unknown to Shura, she had arranged for this impromptu solo performance of the hat dance by Shura and her partner, whom she convinced to partake in this performance. Miguel was too old to enroll in the classes but volunteered as an instructor. It was obvious to Richard that he excelled as a performer.

Shura and Miguel's eyes were locked together as they concentrated on their dance. Richard hoped Michael experienced the same pleasure he did watching Shura dance. Her performance and that of her partner were uplifting, transcending the grief and tragedy of sorrow, hate, and embitterment that he knew she must have experienced as a soldier. Today she was a beautiful young woman dancing to express her joy in living and love, dancing for her beloved. Neither Michael nor Richard would soon forget her performance. When the music ended and the dancers came close together, hidden from the audience by the large sombrero held by Miguel in a simulated kiss, the audience exploded into a standing ovation. It was only then that Richard believed Shura realized that she and Miguel had actually given a solo performance. The other dancers surrounded them and then formed into a line to perform their bows while the audience applauded.

The applause ended when Juanita entered the stage and addressed the crowd.

"Ladies and gentlemen, I promised to introduce you to my dear friend whose performance she was so gracious in sharing with us tonight. But first let me introduce you to her partner, Mr. Miguel Orozco, who some of you may recognize as an All-American first baseman on the national championship University of Arizona baseball team. Miguel has been with us as a student since he was eight years old. After graduation from high school, he continues to volunteer as an instructor. I believe you will agree with me that he is a superb *folklórico* dancer."

The audience again gave a standing ovation to the young dancer, who bowed and swept his sombrero in front of him in gratitude. At that time, Shura extended both her hands to him, drawing him close and kissing him briefly on each cheek. Richard looked around him at the audience. When the performance had first begun, the auditorium was a little over half filled. It was now completely filled, and people were standing in the back. It was obvious to him that many were here for other activities but had been drawn to the auditorium by the music and applause.

"Ladies and gentlemen, I am honored to introduce you to my dear friend Shura Vega. Shura was born and raised in Mexico City but after high school came to the University of Arizona, where she received her education degree. She then traveled to Israel, where she became a citizen and served in the army. She later spent time in Iraq. She has returned to Tucson for a brief visit to reacquaint herself with her soon-to-be father-in-law with her fiancé, Michael Valencia. The couple will be leaving Tucson in a few days to visit her family in Mexico City, where they will formally announce their engagement to her family and friends.

"Because it had been so long since Shura had performed *folklórico*, we concentrated on the two dances you just enjoyed. We also asked Miguel to help us, which he readily agreed to do. We are going to let Shura join her fiancé and family in the audience while we complete the remainder of our performance. Ladies and gentlemen, again, please express your enjoyment for Shura and Miguel's performance."

The audience again rose to their feet and vigorously applauded as the two women embraced, and Miguel escorted Shura to the side of the stage. She soon appeared, still in costume to join Michael. The lady sitting next to Richard quickly volunteered her seat so that Shura could sit next to them.

After the performance, they accompanied Shura to the dressing room, where she exchanged her costume for her street clothes. After an extended farewell greeting to each student performer, Rhonda Golden, and Juanita, they returned home. Richard had prepared a dinner of spaghetti with wine. The four of them shared a leisurely dinner. After dinner, Shura started to help clean the dishes, but Richard insisted that she and Michael retire for the evening. He knew that they still had planning and preparations to complete prior to traveling to Mexico City. Janet insisted that she would help Richard.

After the chores were completed, Richard poured Janet and himself each a glass of Chianti from dinner.

"Richard," Janet said as she sat next to him on the couch, "I can't tell you how much I have enjoyed this evening. You have a wonderful family."

"Thanks, Janet," he replied with a smile.

"There is still this deep-seated need in me to have you help me get a better understanding of your work on the origin of religion. I don't want to discuss it tonight after a perfect day, but I hope you and I can have this discussion soon."

"How about after Michael and Shura leave for Mexico City, you spend an afternoon here on your day off and I'll fix you a nice dinner in the evening? We should be able to cover a lot, undisturbed by the outside world."

"I would love it! Better yet, I'll fix you dinner!"

CHAPTER THIRTEEN

ATONEMENT

It had been two days since Michael and Shura departed for Mexico City. Richard picked up the telephone and called Janet.

"Hello. Janet speaking."

"Janet, Richard. Tomorrow is Wednesday. I think you said that you're off Wednesday and Thursday of this week. Is that correct?"

"Yes."

"May I pick you up tomorrow about midmorning? I have a couple of errands to run, but I should be through by then. Then we can return here and have that discussion you've been asking me about. I'll fix us a dinner, and we can enjoy the evening together."

"I'd love to, Richard. Let me drive to your house. I want to stop by the grocery store and pick up a few ingredients. Remember, I said that I would make you dinner. I just need you to light the grill. I'm going to prepare Chateaubriand. I will also pick up a robust California Cabernet Sauvignon to go with it. Dessert will be a surprise."

"You've got it, Janet. I'm looking forward to tomorrow."

"I am as well. Until tomorrow, Richard."

The next morning, Richard awoke with anticipation of seeing Janet. He was uncertain where his relationship with Janet was going, but he was certain that he wanted to see her again and share her thoughts. He thought about her as he finished cleaning the kitchen after breakfast and prepared the grill for tonight. He was looking forward to sharing this day with her. She was vibrant, curious, and filled with optimism and hope. Her joie de vivre made coping with Jane's death bearable. Her death had affected him more than he had initially realized.

Intellectually, he knew that death was inevitable and that the great majority of people could not select the time and place of their death. Emotionally, he had more difficulty accepting it. Jane had known that her death was approaching. She had been at peace with it. Richard felt no fear or great anxiety about his death, but he wondered about what was on the other side. He had deeply loved Catherine, and her unexpected death at such a young age just a few years into their marriage had devastated him. At least he had been convinced the future for him was bleak without his wife and daughter. He had recovered, especially with the passage of time but, more importantly, when Rachel had unexpectedly come into his life. He had not been looking for another wife or woman, but she came to him with such energy and love that he fell deeply in love with her. She had given him a renewed reason for living and loving. Plus, the two beautiful children they had together brought great pleasure and joy to them both. Rachel had been gone for seven years. He had initially suffered anxiety and foreboding when he first learned of her diagnosis of breast cancer. The following months, which were deeply emotional for him, had at least given him a modicum of hope that she would beat her affliction. His optimism that they would find a cure gradually diminished to acceptance of her death and the desire to make her life as comfortable as possible and to protect her and care for her as best he could. Rachel and Jane had both accepted their impending death with courage and hope. What both women had in common was their deep faith, one Christian and the other Jewish.

Janet, however, was an avowed atheist. Yet she seemed to be deeply grounded in the purpose of her life. Or was she? He would soon find out this afternoon when she arrived.

He walked to the desk with his computer on it and typed the word "atheist" into the search engine. Several entries appeared on the screen. He looked at the clock in the kitchen. He had about fifteen minutes before she arrived. He sat and read. Many definitions described an atheist as someone who doesn't believe in a god or gods. Some definitions discussed the difference between a *theist*, who believes God involves Himself with humanity, and a *deist*, who believes God was the Creator, who, once the universe was created, did not involve Him or Herself in its evolution.

I'll just have to wait and see what Janet has to say.

Richard heard Janet's car pull into the driveway. Her Hyundai had a characteristic sound that announced her arrival. He walked to the car to help with the groceries she had told him she would bring.

"How are you today, Richard?" she asked.

"Never better," he replied.

"Never better?" she asked. "Richard, I'm so happy that you feel that way."

"I was being just a little sarcastic, Janet. Years ago, when I was much younger, I learned that when most people greeted you with such a question, they were being polite or, at most, expected a brief answer like 'good' or even 'great.' However, some folks took it literally and would then give a lengthy discussion of what ails them. I myself was guilty of that after Catherine passed. I soon realized that with rare exceptions, people really did not intend for me to get into a lengthy discussion of my problems. So with a little bit of sarcasm, I sometimes answer 'never better.' That seems to keep the initial greetings short and manageable.

"Here, let me place these into the fridge until we're ready to begin dinner."

"I got it, the 'never better' part," she replied.

"OK, I know you like ice tea. Why don't you pour us both a glass and we'll go into the family room for our talk?"

After they were seated, Richard began to speak, but Janet raised a finger in a silent command for him to wait and to listen.

"Richard, I've briefly told you about myself that I was born into a fundamentalist Protestant family. I'm not sure if other Protestants consider the Church of Christ's Covenant a mainline Christian church in the way they believe they are Christian, but that is not important. I was brought up to believe that by the very fact I was born, I was destined for the terrible fires of hell because of the original sin. We literally believed in the biblical story that because Adam and Eve sinned, we were doomed to suffer eternal punishment unless we accepted Jesus as our savior. I considered myself to be a pretty normal girl, but the yoke of this belief was always on my mind. For example, if I wanted to be pretty, then I was vain, guilty of a sin for which I could be punished. As I got older, I was taught more about God, the God of the Bible who would slaughter whole tribes of people who didn't worship Him either by war, plagues, or terrible catastrophes of fire and brimstone. I was also taught that God was a loving and forgiving God unless you didn't believe or conform to His commandments, then it was eternal hell fire. That was strong motivation to live according to His law.

"I was taught and believed that because we were born into sin and destined for damnation unless we accepted Jesus as our savior, we were corrupt and therefore couldn't trust our thoughts and desires unless they were in line with God's Word. How did we know this? We knew it because the Bible told us so. We never asked, 'Which Bible?' We never asked, 'Where did the Bible come from?' We were simply taught that the Bible was the true Word of God. Later, I learned there are other bibles or at least other interpretations of it. How do we know whose interpretation of it is the true one? Which interpretation of it should we believe? It is absolutely critical to our eternal salvation that we get it right.

"By the time I was sixteen, I began to have doubts about certain things. I wasn't ready to question the most fundamental of the beliefs I had been taught, just the small little things that affected and distressed me as a healthy teenage adolescent girl who was looking for love and happiness. As an aside, it was at this time that I had a relationship with a boy. I had a terrible crush on him, and I believe he felt essentially the same way. One night I lied to my parents about spending the evening with a girlfriend to study when I really intended to meet him. He was old enough to have a driver's license, and he had borrowed the family car. We drove to a secluded spot along a lake that other teenagers used as a 'parking' spot to 'make out' and 'neck.' Things soon got out of control, and we had sex. You can imagine that we were not knowledgeable. We were awkward, and at best, it was less than an experience that made the earth move under my feet, so to speak. But the real consequence of my action began to overwhelm me with fear and remorse. I had sinned. If my parents were ever to find out, I don't know how they would have reacted, but I expected the worse. I don't think they would have disowned me or kicked me out of the house, but I certainly feared that possibility.

"Later, in conversations with my mother, I told her about a friend of mine at school who had done what I had done. Her reaction convinced me that I would never confess to her. She told me not to associate with that 'girl' because she was certain she would suffer damnation for all eternity unless she repented. She looked at me as if she perhaps understood that I was really telling her about myself, although she never said those words. What she did say was don't let a boy send you to hell for a few minutes of pleasure.

"Apparently, she discussed my conversation with my father and later told me that they both agreed I would not be allowed to date boys until I was much older. She told me to concentrate on being with my girlfriends. I not only prayed for forgiveness, but I also foreswore any further relationship with boys. It was at this time I became friends with a girl down the street from a Catholic family. She was beautiful in a very feminine way. We became very close and spent as much time together as we could. She was very affectionate, always hugging me and kissing me on the cheeks. One evening we were at her house. Her parents were away at her brother's baseball game. She began to touch me and stroke my hair. When she began to fondle my breasts, I responded with an almost overwhelming desire to hold her and to kiss her. She was very gentle unlike the boy of my first sexual encounter. She led me into her bedroom, and we lay in bed, kissing passionately and fondling each other. I totally surrendered to her, and when she performed oral sex on me, the earth literally did move. It was from that time until I was a mature woman and lay with you that I knew I was a lesbian. I was happy being a lesbian. We continued to have a deeply personal relationship. She told me that her mother knew she was lesbian. She had told her right after puberty. Her father and brother didn't know. Neither did the rest of the family with the exception of one aunt, her mother's sister, who also knew. After high school, she went away to a Catholic girl's school. We initially kept in touch but eventually drifted away. By this time, I was in my early twenties and questioning everything that I had been taught.

"When I told my mother I wanted to go away to college, she and my father were adamant that I could only attend college if it was a church school recommended by our church since our congregation was too small to have one and was only more or less loosely affiliated with a larger religious association. They said they would consider a local community college. It was at that time that I kissed my parents goodbye, telling them that I would love them forever but that I simply had to leave home to find my way into the world. I did so. The details of my struggles in finding work and attending school are too lengthy to go into now, but suffice it to say a turning point in my life was when I decided I wanted to be a nurse and work in the missions in Africa, even though it cost me the only true relationship I had ever known, the one with whom I believed would be my future wife. After I made that decision, I applied and was accepted to nursing school. After I received my degree, I heard about the university hospital offering signing bonuses to nurses because they were so desperately in need of qualified nurses. I moved to Tucson, met Aaron Silver, and joined the atheist association. There is more to this story, but now is not the time to continue. Then I met you."

She stopped speaking and sipped her tea, not looking at him for several seconds.

"Thank you for sharing that with me, Janet. I can better understand what you've dealt with."

"Did you have a good childhood?"

"Yes. Both my parents were from Southern Arizona and met in high school. I was the younger of two children. My sister is three years older than I. My father joined the navy and made it his career. We spent almost his entire career on the East Coast. I have family here in Arizona, but we really didn't stay in close contact with them. That was one of the reasons I returned to Arizona when my first wife, Catherine, unexpectedly died. My father told me about a great-grandfather—I'm not sure how many greats he is removed from me—who left his home in Caborca, Sonora, Mexico, as a fourteen-year-old teenager for the goldfields of California during the gold rush. That was in 1849 when California had just recently become part of the United States after the Mexican War. He had to travel the infamous El Camino del Diablo or the Devil's Highway to do so. He actually survived and did pretty well becoming an American citizen and a prosperous landowner. My father and I always planned to make the trek together in honor of our intrepid ancestor and to better understand what he faced. Unfortunately, my father passed before we ever had an opportunity to do so together. After Catherine and our two-year-old daughter, Bernadette, died, I was at a loss. I sold the house and came to Arizona to trek the Devil's Highway as sort of tribute to my dad and as a metaphor of my own quest for what I was going to do with the rest of my life. It was during this time that I met Rachel, my second wife, and Michael and Sarah's mother."

"How did your first wife and daughter die?"

"She and Bernadette were in the house, waiting for a playdate with a neighbor and her daughter, when Catherine suffered a ruptured brain aneurysm and collapsed unconscious. Apparently, Bernadette, who was only two years old, became upset and wandered into the backyard. We had a locked gate and fence around the swimming pool, but apparently, it was not properly latched. Bernadette fell into the pool and drowned. When the neighbor came over, she called 911, but the paramedics could not revive Bernadette. They rushed Catherine to the hospital, but she died not long after being admitted to the emergency room."

"Oh my god, Richard, that is so sad. Where were you when this happened?"

"I was deployed on an aircraft carrier in the Persian Gulf. I was a naval flight officer and crewman in the back seat of a Super Hornet fighter attack aircraft. The navy sent me home as quickly as possible. I just didn't have the desire to continue on active duty after it happened, so I requested release and assignment to the reserves."

They were both silent for several seconds. He could not help but notice the way she looked at him.

"So we've both exchanged a little background of our pasts. What would you like to discuss now, Janet?"

"You're right. We should get to the business at hand. Richard, I hope we get to know each other much better. I would like to learn more about you, your family, and everything you would like to share. But let me begin.

"After I lost my faith in God, I, of course, sought something to replace it with. Fortunately, there are several writers who have written about their own personal experiences with the loss of their faith. Some, of course, had never believed in God from early adolescence, but many others were like me, raised in a family with a strong belief in their faith, mostly Christian, but also, some I knew were Jewish. I suppose there are others. I've heard about Muslims who have become atheists as well but not many. Many of these people are good writers who have chronicled their experiences. Some are women like me but unlike me have been able to write eloquently about their life. I have drawn inspiration from their writings and from the discussions and proceedings of the Arizona Atheists Association.

"When I read the draft of your work on the origin of religion, I was struck that what I had previously believed was a superstitious belief in God. That belief was founded in tribal society and was, in reality, actual physical events that occurred in the historical memory of mankind and not really that long ago. I can't tell you how uplifting it was to me to finally be able to see beyond the stories of creation and tribal religion to perhaps a scientific explanation for physical events that had a significant part in the origin of religion. Of course, your draft led me to Velikovsky and also to the electric universe, which provided even more understanding to me."

"Keep one thing in mind, Janet. Science itself is still struggling to accommodate itself to Velikovsky and the work to date that he inspired. One of the greatest thinkers of the twentieth century, I believe, was Albert Einstein. Almost everyone has heard of his theories of relativity. What a lot of people don't know is that Einstein was mistaken in much of his theory, not because he was not consistently brilliant in constructing his theory or theories but because he was forced to make assumptions, which, although appeared reasonable and valid at the time, have been proven to be wrong. No matter how brilliant his theories were, they were not correct because his assumptions were wrong.

"In preparation for our discussion today, I did a little research on several Jewish websites. One I found interesting was about astrology because I remember reading previously that there is a tradition in Judaism about astrology. The bottom line of what

I found is that astrology has something to tell us, but we must follow Halacha in order for it to do us any good. I am greatly oversimplifying what is a complex religious discussion, but the point I wanted to make is that at the beginning of the discussion, the writer, a rabbi, stated words to the effect that *it is an undisputed fact that the universe is expanding.* That is scientifically proven not to be so, but he is stating the conventional wisdom of mainstream science. In order to understand the origin of religion, one has to understand the science behind the events in nature that were significant in the creation of the stereotypes that still reside in the collective unconscious even today. Current mainstream science is woefully inadequate to do so. You said that you had previously read about the electric universe theory?"

"Yes. You mentioned it several times in your draft, and I was curious. I haven't done an in-depth study, but I have read several papers on Internet websites and understand basically what underlies it."

"Can I ask you what you think that is?"

"Of course, you can! The underlying assumption behind mainstream science is that gravity is the fundamental force in the universe that drives and shapes it. But beginning with Velikovsky, we have learned that it is the electromagnetic force that is the force that drives and shapes the universe. You put it very clearly in your draft that the electromagnetic force is greater than the force of gravity by a factor to the thirty-ninth power, which is many times greater than gravity. I know you cite the work of Velikovsky and others whose work you draw on, but the way you described it was very easy for me to understand.

"Thank you. I'm indebted to the scientists and other scholars who have been working to develop this paradigm. What's more, their work is an interdisciplinary effort because this concept of the electric universe explains much more than just cosmology. It is this interdisciplinary synthesis that leads to the search for the origin of religion with a reasonable chance to learn about it. I believe it will eventually lead to a compliance of science, myth, and religion. It is important to understand this force. Do you remember what I summarized about the standard model of particle physics?"

"Yes. You wrote and many other writers whose works I've read also describe that there are four forces: the strong nuclear binding force, the weak nuclear binding force, the electromagnetic force, and gravity. I distinctly remember a wow moment when you cited work by Thornhill in which he states that there probably is only one force, the electrostatic force, and that gravity is probably part of it. I thought it clever of you when you quoted the *Star Wars* greeting of 'May the Force be with you.'"

"I can't take credit for that, but whoever originated it was right on. Do you remember what I wrote in the draft about Velikovsky's theory that Earth was originally part of a brown dwarf system consisting of a binary star system of Saturn and Jupiter with Venus, Earth, and Mars?"

"Yes. It was your summation of Velikovsky's theory that it was the capture of this binary system by our current solar system that started the change, the sequence of events, events that not only shaped and rearranged our solar system but also whose cataclysmic and catastrophic effects on earth caused mankind to tremble in fear. It is in that ancient time in which the archetypes of religion and astrology were implanted into the human psyche and which still affects mankind today. Am I correct?"

"Yes," he replied.

"When I read that, I immediately went to my Bible and turned to Revelations. I remember reading a verse in there years ago that resonated with me when I was undergoing my loss of faith. Do you remember the verse in Revelations 22:17 to be exact? I have memorized it. 'And the Spirit and the bride say, Come. And let him that heareth say, Come. And let him that is **athirst** come. And whosoever will, let him take the water of life freely.' There are other verses in both the Old and New Testaments that speak to hunger and thirst for faith or for righteousness or for salvation.

"Like the Israelites who supposedly wandered in the wilderness for forty years, I also hunger and thirst for something to believe in, something that was not based on superstition and religion. When I first read your draft and your hypothesis about the origin of religion, I was struck with an intense emotional epiphany that truth had been revealed to me. It was similar to what I read in the Bible about being touched by the Lord and stricken with great truth. It has changed my life, Richard. I no longer have to decide between two choices: one, that there is a Creator whose commandments we must obey in order to avoid eternal damnation, or two, the knowledge that whatever the ultimate nature of the universe is, God is immanent in it. But immanence doesn't necessarily mean He is involved in human affairs. It means that however we perceive the universe, that perception or belief shapes our religious faith. I now realize that if we can understand the origin of religious belief and thought, then we can begin to see the forest through the trees. With this truth, I can now turn to the wisdom of philosophers and thinkers, including those of the Eastern religions, to seek further enlightenment. I no longer have to choose between a bleak and unsatisfying belief in atheism or in a terrible and avenging God whose love and faith is predicated on keeping the commandments. I am reminded of the passage in Psalms that I have come to know well. 'The fool has said in his heart there is no God.' It is like I have been wandering in the desert for all these past years, and suddenly, the Almighty has touched my eyes and has given me the ability to more clearly see the way and to seek Him, whatever He may be."

"I am having my own moment of enlightenment, Janet. Since you are so motivated to pursue your recently gained knowledge, why don't you work with me in this compilation? Nothing demands that you must understand something thoroughly before you can attempt to write about it than what we've been discussing."

"You realize, Richard, that I have spent the several past years working to become a nurse in an overseas mission in Africa?"

"Yes. I must ask that you think seriously about what I offer. Stay here and work with me. We can learn much together, and two people doing research and corroborating sources can be a powerful force."

Richard stopped speaking and looked at her.

"What else, Richard?"

"I think I am falling in love with you, Janet. You are a beautiful and desirable woman. I don't mean you are physically beautiful only, which you are, but you have a beautiful mind and spirit, or let me just say it. You have a beautiful soul. I know in my heart that we are destined to be soulmates."

"Are you sure, Richard? I may never step into a church or a synagogue with you. Then again, there is much beauty in ritual and religious tradition once you can understand its human evolution in understanding the world and universe that we live in. It seems strangely appealing to me to be able to engage in ritual without the fear of the fires of hell waiting for me if I stumble over the Ten Commandments."

"Try keeping 613 mitzvoth! I've mentioned before that I've never been what I consider to be a pious or observant Catholic or Jew. But I enjoy my religion, and I am glad that my children were raised in a religious tradition. I believe it grounds them as well as me."

Janet stood and walked to him, kneeling in front of him. She took his hands into hers and began to softly speak as tears welled up in her eyes.

"Richard, meeting you has forever changed my life. The understanding I have achieved through you will guide me in the coming years. I have to tell you that I am engaged to a wonderful woman. Her name is Bethany Maggiore. She is a doctor of neuropathology at the university hospital. She was devastated when I told her about you. I tried to dry her tears and tell her that I was almost certain that my affection for you was as an individual that had given me a different way of looking at my life, my future, and even my relationship with her. I was sure that I loved her truly and would be faithful to her forever after our marriage but that I had to be sure. She is an intelligent woman, brilliant in my opinion. She agreed and told me to do this, and she would wait for me. I am so glad that she did that because now I am certain that she is the one true love in my life and that I can't even contemplate living without her. But I have no regrets knowing you as I did. You will forever hold a special place in my heart, and I will forever be grateful to you for what you have done for me.

"Someday I would like very much for you to meet her, Richard. I think you would come to realize the beautiful person she is. We are truly soulmates. She shares my passion for someday working in the missions in Africa, although she is like you, a nonparticipating member of her faith."

"What about dinner?" he asked.

"Let me prepare this meal that we can share together. Then I will go back to her and to my life, but it will be a life that is much better and enriched for having known you."

After they had eaten and cleaned up, she prepared to leave.

"Richard, I am in a much better place now, and my life is more focused. What about you?"

"I'm not sure," he replied. "Don't worry about me. I will be fine."

She kissed him softly on his lips.

"Goodbye," she said as she walked to her car.

He watched until she had driven out of sight.

CHAPTER FOURTEEN

QUINCEAÑERA

Richard had just returned from retrieving the morning newspaper from the plastic bin mounted on a pole next to the mailbox. He tucked the paper under his arm and glanced to the north. There had been an unusual cold front that had passed over Tucson, yesterday afternoon and last night, which deposited a light dusting of snow in the valley. The peaks on the Catalina Range still were covered in snow and reflected the April sun brightly to those who observed them. Sometimes in early April, an arctic cold front would come barreling through Southern Arizona, bringing with it a welcome delay of the inevitable hot weather that followed in May. Maybe this would postpone the one-hundred-degree days by a week or so in late May. He knew that June would bring its traditional hot days sometimes averaging over a hundred degrees Fahrenheit before the summer monsoon rains came. He took a moment to stand where he was gazing at the mountain while reflecting briefly on the previous several weeks. He had conflicting emotions as he retraced his steps back into the house. He laid the paper on the table next to his recliner and went into the kitchen, where he refilled his coffee mug with the hot dark liquid. He sat in the recliner with the mug in his hands and contemplated the sources of his conflicting emotions.

He had begun to fall for Janet. Maybe he should have listened to the inner voice that had told him to proceed with caution that night he had met her at the Mountain View Cafe and had taken her home. No, he had no regrets. He was glad that she considered his work meaningful to her. He was a better man for knowing her and sharing love, however briefly, with her. He had loved Janet for the person she was. She was truly a beautiful woman both in body and soul. He smiled at how she would understand the statement that she had a soul. That probably was part of her epiphany, that she truly had a soul with which she would seek greater understanding and share her love with another. Yes, he was sad. Yes, he was hurt, but that was sometimes the price of loving a woman. He was a better man for her love. He truly wished the best for her and Bethany and hoped that they would find happiness. Perhaps one day she would face her inevitable death with a better understanding of life and its meaning.

He smiled when his thoughts turned to his son and daughter-in-law. He had flown to Mexico City with his daughter and her family to participate in the wedding. He had truly enjoyed the marriage with all its preparations and joy. Shura's family was remarkable, and their great joy for their returning daughter and her marriage was boundless. Richard wasn't sure just how much her parents realized the tremendous danger Shura had volunteered for in her career as a soldier for both the Israeli army and the Peshmerga. Whether or not they understood, they all shared in the happiness of the marriage and its celebration. His daughter, Sarah; her husband, Drew; and their three children were warmly welcomed by Shura's family and friends.

Michael and Shura were on their honeymoon. They would spend several days in a ski lodge in Colorado. They both had told him that the long months in the desert had made them both yearn for cold and snow and sitting by the fireplace at night, not to live in permanently, they had both reassured him, but for an ideal honeymoon.

Richard was happy that they would be returning to Tucson while Michael pursued an MBA. They both agreed that they could reduce their expenses by staying with him in the guesthouse. Richard was happy to have his son and daughter-in-law nearby.

Now what? he thought. He had almost completed the beginning Hebrew class at the university and had written five more chapters on his draft and was now satisfied that he was nearly finished. He should be satisfied with his life, but there was an emptiness that yet remained within him. He had known it only briefly after Catherine had died, but it had lingered for years after Rachel had passed. Perhaps he would take Naomi Sverdlov's offer of returning to Jerusalem to pursue his work. Certainly, there were more resources in Israel than in Tucson. What would it be like to again travel the Judean hills with Naomi with his newly found understanding of the God of Israel?

He turned to place the mug on the table next to the recliner, and as he did so, he noticed that there was a digital message on the screen, indicating a missed call. Curious, he picked the receiver from its cradle and dialed in the number to retrieve the voice mail.

"Richard, this is Arnold Rocha. I just found out from Angelica that you were here in Tucson. It's been, what, about twenty or so years since we've seen each other? I retired from my law practice because of my mother's health. I've been her caregiver for the last five years. She recently passed. I was having dinner with Angelica, and she mentioned to me that she had recently seen you at the Jewish Community Center for a student *folklórico* concert. She didn't get a chance to speak to you, but she thought that I might be interested in contacting you. Listen, give me a call when you can. I'd like to get together with you for lunch and talk about old times. My number is on your answering machine. Hope you're doing well."

Lt. Arnold Rocha had been a JAG officer assigned to Naval Air Station Oceana when he had been on active duty. Richard had been squadron ordnance officer when his weapons crew was being evaluated for safety procedures during loading and removing ordnance on the Super Hornet. Richard remembered that it was early morning on a bitter cold and rainy day with sleet and light snow falling on the crew as they worked. One of the handling crew, an aviation ordnanceman, had been injured when he slipped on the icy tarmac during transfer of an air-intercept missile to the wheeled gurney. Because the petty officer had broken his ankle, the commanding officer directed that Richard, a lieutenant junior grade at the time, conduct a JAG[21] investigation. It was Richard's first JAG investigation, so he had intensely studied the JAG manual to ensure he followed correct procedure. He called the air station's legal office and asked to speak to a JAG officer with some questions that he was unsure of after reading the manual several times. It was at that time that he had met Arnold Rocha. They eventually became friends. Arnold had enlisted in the navy after graduating from the University of Arizona and had been accepted to the Navy's Law Education Program after completing two years at the university's law school. After commissioning as a reserve officer, he had completed the program and had been awarded his juris degree. His first assignment had been at Naval Air Station Oceana, and from there, he had served in Hawaii at the JAG office of COMPACFLT or the commander of the U.S. Pacific Fleet. He had been released from active duty after his obligatory service was over.

Richard had lost contact with Arnold until he worked as a private contractor for a company with a navy contract to develop a missile similar to the Phoenix missile that the F-14 Tomcat had carried. At the time, the Chinese were building a modern blue-water navy and were developing a sea-airborne attack capability against U.S. Navy aircraft carriers. The navy had not replaced

[21] Judge Advocate General's Corps (JAG Corps), the legal arm of the United States Navy.

the Phoenix missile with a similar capability after the Tomcat had been retired from service. The navy strategic planners had grown extremely concerned about the lack of an effective air counter threat to the planned Chinese missile and had awarded a contract to a private company to develop such a capable missile. Because Richard had only been recently released from active duty after he lost his first wife, Catherine, he was contacted by a friend and former Super Hornet pilot who was now working as the company's civilian test pilot flying Super Hornets on loan from the navy. Richard and he had been crewed for several months, flying combat over Iraq and Afghanistan. He had accepted the company's offer to work as a subcontractor in the test and evaluation phase of the missile before turning the product over to the navy. He spent several weeks in Los Angeles flying the Super Hornet out of the Los Angeles International Airport or LAX while conducting the airborne test and evaluation phase. He had taken Rachel, his second wife, with him several times, and it was during one of these visits that he had looked up Arnold Rocha.

At the time, Arnold had built a successful law practice as an injury attorney. After his release from the navy, Arnold had settled in Los Angeles and had worked for a law firm until he passed the California bar. During this time, he had been working as a criminal defense lawyer and told Richard that he would often receive calls in the early morning hours from clients who had been arrested and asked to be bailed out. He had quickly grown tired of his criminal practice and, after some research on the potential of the Los Angeles market, discovered that there were several hundred thousand Mexicans or Mexican Americans in the greater metropolitan area. At that time, there were very few Hispanic attorneys serving that huge market. Most injury lawyers were Anglo. He had changed his name to Arnoldo Rocha and had taken several intensive Spanish courses until he could speak, understand, and write it fluently. His law practice had thrived and had made him a great deal of money. Richard suspected that he was a millionaire, but Arnold was always reluctant to talk about the details of his wealth.

He and Rachel had also met Angelica Delacruz during several of their visits to Los Angeles. Angelica had attended Tucson High and the university with Arnold. She had received her master's degree in education and had also left Tucson for Los Angeles. Arnold had dated her in high school, and they had reestablished their relationship in Los Angeles, although after two years of dating, they had gone their separate ways. Richard had not had contact with either one for the last twenty or thirty years.

He returned Arnold's phone call, and they agreed to meet for lunch at La Taqueria Grande located west of Interstate 10 on Grande Avenue between Speedway Boulevard and Congress Street.

Richard left his home at eleven fifteen. He figured it was about seventeen miles from his house to the restaurant, and he didn't want to be late. It was a Wednesday, and at that time of the day, traffic would not be a problem. He remembered the first time he had driven into this part of Tucson from Gila Bend thirty-one years ago. It was two days before he met Rachel. He experienced a feeling of sadness and nostalgia as he crossed the interstate and turned south from Speedway onto Grande Avenue. He made a left turn from Grande into the parking lot of the restaurant. He saw Arnold as he entered the covered patio in front of the entrance. Arnold no longer sported the jet-black hair he remembered. He was now mostly white and gray highlighted by several dark strands. He also sported a white beard and mustache.

Arnold stood and smiled as he approached, extending his hand, and greeted him warmly, "Hello, Richard. It's good to see you again. It's been a long time."

"It has, Arnold. It's good to see you as well. I hope you're in good health. You look good."

"We'll talk about that later. Look at us! Two *viejos, dos barbas grises!*"

"It amazes me how fast time passes. Shall we go inside and get a table?"

"Yes. This restaurant is not upscale, but the Mexican food is superb."

After they were served, they spoke of what had occurred in their lives since their last meeting in Los Angeles twenty years ago. Arnold was saddened to hear about the loss of Richard's second wife. He never knew or met Catherine, even though they had been stationed together at Oceana. He did fondly remembered Rachel since they had met for dinner several times during Richard's working visits to Los Angeles.

"Rachel was also an attorney, wasn't she? I remember now that she was an immigration attorney and was doing some pro bono work for an organization called La Gente Eligida. I never knew until several days ago when I had dinner with Angie Delacruz and she told me about you. Do you remember Angie? Her friends have always called her Angie, but her name is Angelica. Delacruz is her maiden name. We dated for about two years then separated, although we have always kept in contact as friends. She's been married and divorced twice but has always taken back her maiden name."

"I remember meeting Angie once in LA during dinner at a restaurant in Santa Monica. I remember her as an attractive woman and very intelligent. She was a schoolteacher, wasn't she?"

"Yes. She was one of many Mexican American women who had to leave for California after getting their teaching degree because there was an inherent bias against hiring them by the Anglos who ran the school districts. She's retired now and has been back in Tucson for several years. When she saw you at the Jewish Community Center, she said you were with your son and his fiancée. Apparently, his fiancée participated in part of the dancing, and the MC who is also a friend of hers explained to the audience who she was and why she was in Tucson. It was at that point that Angie saw you and remembered you. She also told me that you have a history in Tucson involving your late wife.

Apparently, she was being stalked and threatened by two rogue Border Patrol officers, and they attempted to kill you and your wife, but your female bodyguard and you shot and killed them both. In the incident, your female bodyguard was also shot and killed. That had to be a tough experience."

"Yes. Neither Rachel nor I ever fully recovered from her loss. Her name was Diedra Gonzalez, and she became a close friend. She was responsible for saving Rachel's life that day. She was young, only about twenty-six years old, when she came to work with us, but she had already accomplished much in her life and was on her way to preparing for the Arizona bar. She considered Rachel as a role model. My wife and she became very close."

"I did a little research on you and the two officers involved. Apparently, they were part of a white supremacy organization, which also involved several prominent people, including some other law enforcement officers. I believe they are still very active in Arizona. Right now, there is a Republican candidate campaigning for president on a semi-nationalist right-wing movement, and he has stirred up a lot of activity among neofascists, Eurocentric organizations, as well as outright white supremacy groups. I'm surprised that they didn't attempt any further action against you or your wife."

"I believe that is true because the two rogue Border Patrol officers were federal officers and the federal investigators conducted an extensive and thorough investigation. One of the local newspaper reporters who just happened to be present at the incident was able to get a copy of the investigative report after overcoming several delays and obstacles and published it. Some of the prominent folks and their relationship to some of the organizations were then widely known, and I believed this served as a deterrent for further actions against us by these assholes."

"We can talk about this further, Richard, if you want, but I sense it's still somewhat painful for you. Listen, let me change the subject. I mentioned to Angie that I would be meeting you today for lunch, and she asked me to invite you to her house. One of her niece's daughters is having her *quinceañera* this Saturday, and she wanted me to invite you and any lady friend you may want to bring. Are you interested?"

"Yes. As a matter of fact, I've been thinking I need to get out and socialize more. I don't have a lady friend, so I'll just come by myself."

"Great! I would guess that there will be some unattached women there. Who knows? Maybe you'll meet someone."

"Thanks, Arnold, but I'd just as soon not get involved with a woman right now. I do have one project I'm working on."

"I'd love to hear about it. Let's get together for another lunch or even dinner. I do have a doctor's appointment in less than an hour, and although it's not too far from here, I need to get started now. You probably know as well as I that traffic keeps getting worse in Tucson."

***

Richard left home at twelve thirty on Saturday afternoon for the *quinceañera*. He drove west on Fifth Street and turned south onto Avenida Histórica in the Sam Hughes neighborhood, where Angelica Delacruz's house was located. He noticed a large sign that read,

> *Welcome to the Sam Hughes Neighborhood*
> *Designated as an Historic Neighborhood*
> *On the National Register of Historic Places*
> *Built and developed from 1920 through 1954*
> *Tucson Historic Preservation Office*

Turning west onto College Street, he noticed a dozen cars or so parked on the street in front of a Spanish Colonial Revival house and confirmed by the address that it was Angelica's. He made a U-turn at the next intersection and parked directly in front of the house across the street. There were about four spaces marked by a red ribbon with a hand-painted sign that read Reserved. He assumed the spaces were for the party that had attended the customary *quinceañera* mass and would be returning soon. The house appeared to have been built in the 1920s. It was painted white and had a red clay tile roof. The windows were large and traditional. He noticed that there had been two additions on each side of the house built in the same style. There was also an ornate wrought iron fence embedded in a base of white concrete finished in stucco. The large wrought iron gate was obviously controlled remotely. As he exited the car, he noticed a large sports utility vehicle with several passengers towing a large trailer stop in front of the house and began to discharge several men and women in mariachi costume. He walked across the street and followed the members of the mariachi troupe into the yard and house. Arnold Rocha was greeting them and telling where to set up their instruments and amplifiers. He saw Richard and greeted him warmly.

"Hello, Richard. I'm glad you came. I'm helping Angie in directing folks where to go. Her sister, brother, and a couple of lady friends are actually helping her organize and run the *quinceañera*. She asked me to come early to help out. Let me get the band in position and I'll introduce her to you and show you around."

"Good. Don't worry about me, Arnold. I'll just tag along and stay out of the way."

Richard followed Arnold into the house, which was furnished in a traditional style. Although no expert in furniture, he did recognize two styles that he had learned from Rachel: a pair of beautiful red bergère chairs and an impressive oak dining table with six fauteuil chairs. The house had been remodeled and, although built many years ago, had all the conveniences of a modern home. Before he was able to observe more, he was greeted by an attractive woman of about fifty years. She wore a striking turquoise-and-silver Navajo necklace over her dark long-sleeve blouse and matching ankle-length skirt. Her black hair was liberally streaked with strands of gray-and-white hair, which she had gathered into a twist held by a silver clasp. Her brown eyes accentuated her infectious, welcoming smile as she greeted him.

"You must be Richard Valencia." She smiled as she greeted him, "Welcome to my home. I am so glad you came. It's a pleasure to meet you. Arnold has told me many good things about you."

"You must be Angelica Delacruz," Richard responded, accepting her hand and hug. "Thank you for inviting me. Arnold has also told me many nice things about you."

"We have been friends for a long time. Listen, I've got to take care of a few things right now, but please go into the backyard and have a drink. Arnold will be there soon to introduce you to folks. Thank you for sharing this joyous occasion with us."

"I understand the *quinceañera* is for your great niece. Is that correct?"

"Yes! *Mi gran sobrina* is Estelle Robles, my niece Michelle's daughter. She will be fifteen today, and it's a joyous celebration. Excuse me, Richard. Go! Make yourself at home."

Richard smiled at her as she scurried off to take care of the many demands required of the hostess of such a party. He walked into the beautifully landscaped backyard. There was a large gazebo off to the west and a large smooth-finished rectangular concrete slab that could serve perfectly as a dance floor. There were perhaps twenty or so guests in the yard holding drinks, snacking on hors d'oeuvres, and talking to one another. There were also about fifteen tables covered in white tablecloths with seating for five around the perimeter of the concrete slab. Toward the rear of the yard near the block wall that separated the yard from the back alley, Richard noticed a cottage. There was also one on the eastern side of the yard, slightly larger. Arnold had told Richard that Angelica rented the two cottages to male tenants—one, an older man of about eighty years, who had been her tenant for over twenty years, and another, a black professor of English at the university, who had been with her for five years.

Richard walked to the bar and asked the bartender for *una cerveza fria*. Thanking him, he turned around to see Arnold speaking with an attractive dark-haired woman with beautiful olive skin of about forty years or so. She wore her hair in what Richard thought was a short bob. She was striking in her appearance, and the black blouse she wore over a tan skirt accentuated her figure. Her scoop neckline just tantalizingly hinted at décolletage. Her silver and beaded dangle earrings sensually moved with her head as she looked at Arnold and then occasionally at the people in the yard. Richard approached his friend and the woman, hoping Arnold would introduce her to him. As he approached them, she turned toward him and smiled. Richard returned her smile.

"Richard, let me introduce you to my friend Anita Castellano. Like Angelica, she is a retired schoolteacher. However, she is active in many different endeavors. Anita, this is my good friend Richard Valencia."

"Mucho gusto en conocerlo, Richard." She smiled as she offered him her hand.

"El placer es todo mío de verdad!" Richard replied as he took her hand.

"I've heard quite a bit about you, Richard. Apparently, you have quite a history here in Tucson." Anita smiled as she looked him in the eye.

"I hope at least some of it's been good," he replied casually.

"Listen, you two, please excuse me," Arnold said. "I think the caterers are arriving, and I promised Angie I would supervise their setup and serving when the time comes. Why don't you two keep each other company until this celebration gets started? I'll rejoin you as soon as I can."

"Thanks, Arnold," Anita replied. Turning to Richard, she asked, "Richard, do you mind getting me a frozen margarita? I promised myself one this afternoon, and it's early enough that I can enjoy it without worrying about driving. Make sure it's in the largest glass available."

Richard lifted his beer toward her as if saluting and turned toward the bar to fulfill the lady's request. When he returned to where he had left her, she was not there. He looked around and saw her sitting at a small white wrought iron table set in a shady corner of the yard, almost out of sight from the main yard. She waved at him.

He placed the large glass of frozen margarita with salt rimmed around its edge with lime juice in front of her and sat across the small round table.

"This is a nice spot," he observed. "It's also very quiet and in the shade. Obviously, you must have known its location before because it's not readily visible from the yard."

"Exactly," she replied. "I have a confession to make. When Angie mentioned that she had invited an old friend of Arnold, we both went to our yearbooks to see if we could find you. Of course, we couldn't since you were born and raised on the East Coast. However, one of Angie's friends involved at the *folklórico* concert at the JCC had told us both over lunch about you, your son, and his fiancée. She also said she met you at your house when your son, Michael, and his fiancée, Shura, hosted a barbecue and informal reunion. We, of course, were both extremely curious about you, and we did extensive research to see what we could find about you. One of our close friends, a retired school librarian, works at the *Arizona Daily Observer* as an archivist. We tasked her to search the archives to see what if anything had been written about you."

She stopped speaking and sipped her margarita while looking coyly at him over the glass. After a brief interlude, Richard asked, "What, if anything, did you find?"

"You are more intimately familiar with the details than any of us could ever be. We found out that your late wife was an immigration attorney that did quite a bit of work, including pro bono work, for several organizations that sought to help immigrants. One of those organizations, La Gente Eligida, was founded and run by a good friend of mine who was also a mentor when I was a young volunteer for her organization. Isabella Gutierrez worked with your wife, Rachel Valencia, nee Cohen, and you to assist immigrants who needed financial, moral, and legal assistance. Apparently, a husband of one of your wife's clients was deported. He was trying to illegally reenter the country to rejoin his wife and son when he was shot and killed by a rogue Border Patrol agent and an accomplice, also a rogue agent. The startling and salient fact in the history of that case is that the rogue agent was only one of many others who were members of and supported white supremacy organizations here in the state."

Anita again stopped speaking and took a sip from her margarita. She looked at Richard with her brown and beautiful piercing eyes as if to ask "What are you doing now?"

Richard wasn't sure where Anita's questions were taking the conversation, but he decided to proceed slowly.

"Anita, that was over thirty years ago. We lost a dear friend and beautiful young lady who was Rachel's bodyguard. Neither Rachel nor I ever forgot her actions, which saved our lives, and have always tried to honor her memory in any way we could. But that happened over thirty years ago. Thanks to Diedra Gonzalez, her name, Rachel and I were able to lead a fairly normal life and enjoyed thirty years of marriage. We raised a family of two wonderful children who have been able to achieve rewarding and successful lives. My daughter has given me three beautiful grandchildren, and the way my son, Michael, and his bride are talking, I will soon be given the gift of more grandchildren. I have been content with my life, and since Rachel's passing, I have tried to work in what I consider to be a meaningful pursuit of knowledge. I am currently working on a book I hope to complete within a year. I'm telling you this because I have a feeling, perhaps something in your eyes, that tells me you have brought my past up for a purpose other than idle curiosity."

Richard noticed a slight change of expression on his companion's face, perhaps a slight raising of her eyebrows.

I think maybe his life since his wife's passing was not as content as he would have me believe, she thought before speaking. "I understand that you don't want to talk about the killing of your friend and two rogue agents at this point in time during this happy celebration, but I very much would like to speak with you again about it."

"Why?"

"Because the white supremacy movement, which has always been woven into the fabric of Arizona history and politics, is becoming more threatening to minorities in this country and, in particular, to immigrants. I'm sure you are aware that one of the Republican candidates for president of the United States has become a darling of several hate groups, including the Ku Klux Klan, neo-Nazis, Nazis, Eurocentric protagonists, and white supremacy groups. This collection of similar-thinking groups has been dubbed the 'alt-right.'"

"Why are you telling me this?"

"Because you defended your family and yourself with lethal force, which is your God-given right to do. Even the most ardent redneck of the American Arms Association would agree with that. Richard, I am going to entrust you with something I believe in and support. I trust that you will treat it with the utmost confidentiality and not disclose what I'm about to tell you to anyone without my permission."

"I'm not sure I can agree to such a stipulation. What if I don't agree?"

"I will tell you anyway, and I have complete trust in you to comply with my wishes unless the most extreme circumstances would make my request OBE. I'm sure as a military veteran, you're familiar with that term?"

"Yes. It stands for overcome by events. Why do you place such trust in me?"

"Because I have not only read the federal investigation on the whole sordid affair with the two rogue Border Patrol agents, including their killing of the illegal immigrant who had gestured his surrender and did not oppose arrest. They were found to be guilty of murder, posthumously, of course. You, your wife, and Diedra Gonzalez were found to be innocent of any charges that were brought against you by the preliminary investigation that the journalist you mentioned earlier, Lisa Vargas, had obtained through a Freedom of Information Act request, a request, I might add, that was delayed and extensively redacted. But the findings of the investigation were that you had a right to act as you did.

"Since then, there has been a movement among minorities in general and Mexican and Mexican American minorities in particular to actively pursue defense against discrimination by vigorous means, including voter registration and political participation. There has also been an ongoing discussion about what happened in Germany under the Nazis. Many believe it could also somewhat repeat itself here in the United States."

"I'm not sure I agree, Anita. Germany is not the United States. There are more historical and cultural differences than similarities, I believe."

"I disagree."

They both heard several welcoming comments and congratulations from the people in the yard. The party of relatives and friends who had accompanied the young girl whose *quinceañera* this was returned from mass. The young fifteen-year-old girl dressed in white was surrounded by an admiring group. At that time, the mariachi band began to play.

"I guess we'll have to continue this discussion at some other time. It's now time to join the celebration," Anita said.

"Yes. Actually, there might not be more to discuss. I'm not sure why you are discussing this, although I do admit I find it interesting," Richard replied.

"Listen, Angie said that she learned from Juanita Marques that you are working on a draft of a book about the origin of religion. She also told us that several people who read your work so far spoke highly of it. Please let me give you my e-mail address so that you can attach a copy of what you have done to date. I promise I won't plagiarize any of it. Then you can come over to my house for dinner, and we can continue this interesting conversation. What do you think?"

Richard nodded in agreement and smiled as she reached into a pocket in her skirt and took out a small notepad and pen. She wrote her name, telephone number, and home and e-mail addresses on it and handed it to him.

"We have to join the crowd before they start paging us on the public address system. I'll call you when I receive the e-mail and draft of your work. Then we can set a date to get together. Do you recognize the song?"

"No."

"It's 'El Corrido del Caballo Blanco.' Do you know how to corrido?"

"Yes!" Richard replied as he offered her his arm and led her to the dance floor.

CHAPTER FIFTEEN

LA ROSA BLANCA

Richard set aside his Sunday paper and sipped his coffee. It had been almost a week since he had sent Anita an e-mail with a copy of his work. She would have had time to read it and perhaps research some of the references by now. He smiled as he thought about the attractive dark-haired woman he had met at the *quinceañera*. She had told him that she and Angie had done some research on him personally. He also had picked Arnold's brain to learn more about her. She was forty-eight years old and divorced. She had a daughter who lived here in town. Like Angie, she had received her degree in education at the university and, after teaching for several years, had received her master's in education as well. Like her friend Juanita Marques, she had also been a principal at one of the Tucson Unified School District elementary schools for three years before she had retired just last year. Arnold had mentioned that she had been involved in several endeavors. He learned that some of those were in volunteering to support the children of immigrants in receiving an education. She also continued to volunteer at La Gente Eligida, although since Isabella Gutierrez's passing, that organization had quietly continued its work with immigrants below public scrutiny or controversy.

He closed his eyes and thought again about her after their discussion at the *quinceañera*. She was obviously intelligent and well educated as well as attractive. Actually, he thought she was beautiful with her bobbed black hair and dark brown eyes. Those eyes held a fascination for him. He could not readily discern what she was thinking or her reactions to different statements in their conversation. There was something she had in mind, he knew. He would find out when she called to invite him over for dinner. She had told him she wanted to continue their discussion. He knew it would be something unexpected and it would include him.

Her call came at eleven thirty just as he was thinking about preparing a light lunch.

"Richard, have you had lunch yet?" she asked.

"I was just thinking about preparing something light to eat. Why?"

"I want you to come over for an early dinner. You could even consider it a late brunch. I'm preparing a pot roast. I'd like to eat about three this afternoon. Why don't you come over in an hour or so and we can talk while I finish dinner? If you're hungry, I'll prepare some snacks."

"I'd love to. Give me your address again. I'll be there in an hour. I just need to shower and shave."

"Actually, I live not too far from Angie in the Sam Hughes neighborhood. It's funny how some of us tend to resettle in that area. Of course, it's convenient to downtown and the university. My house is not as large as Angie's, but it suited my daughter and me just fine."

After Richard had written the address, he asked, "Is your daughter still with you?"

"No, she's married and has her own family. They live on the east side of Tucson. Her name is Patricia, and her husband's name is Gordon Billingsly. They're expecting their first child in two months."

"Congratulations on becoming a grandmother!"

"Thank you. Shall I expect you in an hour then?"

"I'll be there."

Richard pulled up to the address she had given him on Eighth Street, a few blocks south from Angie's house. It was similar to Angie's home but without any additions. He noticed that the original windows had been replaced with modern sliding glass panes. The roof was also red tiled. He parked curbside in front of the house and walked to the door and rang the bell. Anita opened the door and greeted him with a smile, *"Bienvenidos. Pase por favor.* I see you didn't have any trouble finding the place. Are those beautiful flowers for me?"

"Yes. I thought perhaps they would add a little color to what I hope is a pleasant Sunday afternoon for you."

"It is! Please come in and make yourself at home while I find a vase to put these flowers in. I'll set them on the table where we can both enjoy them while eating."

"Something smells good in the kitchen," Richard said as he followed her.

After she had placed the vase of flowers on the table, she turned to him.

"Dinner will be ready at three. I've prepared some snacks to munch on if you like, a vegetable plate and dip, a fruit bowl, and the ubiquitous bowl of salted peanuts. I'm about to have a glass of wine. Would you care to join me, or would you prefer a drink or a beer?"

"Wine would be great."

"Red or white?"

"Red."

"I've recently discovered a wonderful dark red blend from a California vineyard that I really like. I'll pour you a glass, and you can tell me what you think."

"Thanks."

After they were seated in the living room, she sat across him. She was wearing what appeared to be a fashionable light pink sweat suit with hand-painted designs on the shirt. She was again wearing dangle earrings, which swayed when she moved her head.

She is a classy lady, he thought.

"So what do you think of my work so far?" Richard asked. "I hope I've made it clear that the tremendous scholarship that it entails is not my original work. I've tried to summarize in one book a great deal of effort that has permitted me to present my thesis that we are at a point in our learning that could lead us to a better understanding of the origin of religion."

"I found it interesting, no, fascinating, Richard. I would imagine that some people would find it objectionable since their faith believes that God Himself has revealed their religion."

"Do you find it so?"

"No. My Catholic faith is unmovable. It doesn't matter to me by what means God has given it to us. I am deeply religious but not publicly. My religion is a deeply personal thing for me. I am sure, however, that there will be many who will appreciate and comment on such a proposal."

"One question, Anita. Do you believe that your Catholic religion is the one true religion and the only way to what Christians believe is salvation?"

"I don't know, nor do I care. If someone believes in their faith, no matter what it is, then that is a good thing. My faith is between God, Jesus, and myself. If I am true to my faith, then I have done what I want and need for salvation. Let me ask you. I have learned from reading about you that you were raised Catholic in a Mexican American family but that you converted to Judaism when you married your late wife. Do you believe that Jesus was the Son of God and that you must accept Him as your savior for salvation?"

"I believe that Jesus was truly a holy man. I don't believe He ever meant for us to believe He was God, the same God who is the Creator of the universe. I believe that He considered Himself on a mission to teach us that the kingdom of heaven was within each of us and we could achieve what we call salvation from within. It is obvious to me from what you've told me that you are a devout and observant Catholic. I wonder if you think the less of me for not being one."

"No, not at all. I meant it when I said my Catholic faith is between me and my God. If God has something else in mind for others, I accept it. I accept it, that is, unless their faith calls for the forced conversion of others to theirs or death to the so-called infidels."

She stopped speaking and looked at him expectantly. He remained silent for a few seconds.

"Is there something else you wanted to discuss?"

"Yes. I alluded to it at the *quinceañera* the other day, but I didn't get a chance to continue. Have you ever heard of an organization called La Rosa Blanca?"

"No."

"I'd be surprise if you did. The White Rose, La Rosa Blanca—if you research the name on the Internet, it will lead you to several things, but two, which are relevant to my discussion, are the names of two women. The first is Lydia Vladimirovna Litvyak or Lilya. She was a female pilot in the Soviet Air Force during World War II and flew sixty-six combat missions before she was killed. She was also the first of two female fighter aces with a total of twelve solo and four shared kills. She was killed at the age of twenty-one during the Battle of Kursk. She was known as the White Rose of Stalingrad because of the White Rose she painted on her plane.

"There is another woman associated with the name of the White Rose. She is Sophie Scholl. The White Rose was a secret nonviolent resistance group founded in Nazi Germany by university students who included Sophie and her brother, Hans Scholl. These young students shared an unbelievable amount of courage and grace to resist Hitler and the Nazis in Germany during the dark years of World War II. Both were executed by the Nazis. Sophie was only twenty-two years when she died.

"Why do I tell you about these two women, the White Rose, and La Rosa Blanca?"

Before he could answer, she continued.

"I spoke briefly about the so-called alt-right the other day. Bear with me while I give some background before I tell you what my association with La Rosa Blanca is. Hate groups, including anti-immigrant groups, have been a part of American history since the founding of the republic and before. Currently, the alt-right is a loose coalition of various racist groups, including the Ku Klux Klan, Neo-Nazis, and other Eurocentrists. They desire that the United States be a white nation through severe restrictions on immigration and eventually through 'ethnic cleansing.' Until they can achieve a white United States, they want to establish Eurocentric zones with borders that preclude other races and ethnicities. They are the spiritual inheritors of those Germans who brought the Nazis to power. These Americans are every bit as capable as those Germans of genocide and unspeakable inhumane acts of terror against those they consider inferior to themselves, to those they consider an obstacle to achieving their white America.

"The German people inflicted such an egregious crime against humanity that it can be universally condemned by the standard that the German philosopher Immanuel Kant set forth in his 'categorical imperative.' Kant was one of the lights of the German Enlightenment, which, by the way, was when your Reform Judaism was founded, I believe. If the German people could inflict such evil on humanity after achieving a government imbued with the principles of the enlightenment, then it can certainly happen here in America. White Americans have already inflicted genocide on Native Americans, and an entire segment of the American body politic established a rebellious government dedicated to the proposition that all men are not created equal but that the white man has the God-given right to dominate and hold in bondage other races. That is also an egregious crime on a par with the Holocaust, in my opinion. You may not yet know that white Americans perpetuated an ethnic cleansing against

Mexicans as well as Mexican Americans during the thirties.[22] These Americans are currently in the minority, but they number in the millions, and as the demographic makeup of this country evolves to a nonwhite majority, their hate and vile actions will only continue to increase."

She paused briefly to take a sip from her wine. Richard knew that she was somewhat animated, but her expression did not indicate it. He realized that she was a highly disciplined woman.

"Richard," she said as she turned toward him with a subtle change of expression that seemed to him to have softened slightly, "I am a woman. Like many, if not most women, I am by nature inclined to nurture. I am a mother who has given birth to a child and nurtured her and protected her to the best of my ability. Fortunately, I do not live, at least not yet, in a society similar to that in which Sophie Scholl lived in her Nazi Germany. I will never be a soldier or a fighter pilot as Lilya was. I have made up my mind that I will prepare myself to resist this evil of racism if it should come to power in this country like the women of the French Resistance did against the occupying German armies. The women of the French Resistance used every means at their disposal to not only resist the Germans but to also effectively kill them with by whatever means available to them. They employed deception and stealth, but if they had to use their feminine beauty for sex, they did, if they had to prostitute themselves to do so, they did with élan and courage.

"There is a small group of us, all women ranging in age from the mid-thirties to late sixties, who have, by whatever means, come together with a common shared interest in nurturing children and helping others less fortunate than ourselves. We have gradually become aware that the level of anti-Semitism and anti-immigration in this country is becoming more prevalent than in past years, and it is in large measure because of the

---

[22] Francisco E. Balderrama and Raymond Rodríguez, *Decade of Betrayal, Mexican Repatriation in the 1930s*, (University of New Mexico Press, Albuquerque, 2006), 1

current political division. We have agreed to participate in such things as political action, education, and voter registration. We have also made the commitment to prepare ourselves to resist by whatever means possible should that become necessary. If the time comes, we will form the core of a woman's resistance that can act either alone or in conjunction with other resistance groups, probably most of which will be formed by men. We include women like me, devout Catholics, but there are women of other faiths, including Protestants and Jews. There is even one Muslim woman, a professor in Islamic studies at the university. She discovered us quite by accident when she was telling a group of women about how she was tortured in her native country as a young girl because she sought an education. We don't discuss religion because most believe that our religion is between ourselves and our God, and while it may motivate us, we will not resist in the name of religion or God but in the decent principles of American democracy. It just does not seem right to kill a fascist for Christ if that is, in fact, what it is. Angie, by the way, is not a member of La Rosa Blanca."

She stopped speaking and sipped wine from her glass, which she held close to her lips as she looked over it at him. Richard also did not speak for several moments.

"I ask again, Anita, why are you telling me this? If you're a devout Catholic, what about the commandment *thou shalt not kill*?"

"Richard, Angie told me that she learned you are taking a Hebrew course at the university to better read your source documents in the original tongue in which they were written. You should probably know that in the Hebrew, the commandment was *thou shalt not murder*, not *thou shalt not kill*. There is not one woman in La Rosa Blanca that ever wants us to have to take action. But it would be a grievous sin not to be prepared to defend ourselves, our children, and our families. We have regularly scheduled firearms training at the municipal firing range south of Tucson. Several of us are also involved in self-defense classes, which have also proven useful for anti-assault and anti-rape defense. Some of our members are instructors for their own religious organization, like our Jewish member. During my studies, I came across a photograph of Eisenhower speaking to American paratroopers who were about to jump behind German lines just prior to the Normandy landing. Recently, when I read about the so-called antifas, I realized that Eisenhower was one, an anti-fascist, and he was speaking to American anti-fascists that were about to wreak incomparable violence in Europe. How much better would it be to kill those comparably few who would plunge us into another violent era before they could do so again? In fact, I believe it is a moral imperative.

"Richard, you have already taken direct action against this evil. You did so to protect your wife and family. The American judicial system found that you were in the right to do so. If this country ever gets a racist president with the power to appoint federal judges who believe as he does, that option for justice may not be available to us. I'm not asking you to do anything. I'm just asking you to think about what I've told you. Hopefully, the time will never come when we need to actively resist, but if it does, I personally will call on you. If that ever happens and if you choose not to do so, you won't ever have to associate yourself with me again."

"You know, I've read a few histories of the Second World War, some of which included information about the French Resistance. There were several instances of cells and individuals that were compromised, arrested, tortured, and executed. What makes you think that might not happen to you, God forbid, if we ever experience what you're preparing for?"

"I am fully aware of that. I wrote my master's thesis on the French Resistance during that war."

"I thought you had a degree in education."

"I do. I graduated from the university with two degrees, education and European history. I was fortunate to also have earned my master's. I understand there is always a risk of compromise, but if and when the time comes, we will have an already existing organization that has been working together for a few years now. I think I read that you were in combat when you were in the navy. Is that correct?"

"Yes."

"Then you knew and accepted the risk of being killed or injured in combat. Yet you still performed your duty. It is the same with us, but our very existence and that of our people, or at least people like us, would be at risk. But even more important, if the racists prevail, this country will not survive as we know and love it."

"Your point is taken."

"Come," she said, "let's eat. I'll pour you a second glass of wine. You can sit down at the table, and I'll serve you."

Dinner was remarkably pleasant. Their conversation concentrated on the weather, the neighborhood, and Tucson in general. Richard did not attempt to bring up any of her previous discussion. He was happy to avoid it altogether. After they had finished eating, she stood and began to clear the table.

"I'll help you," he said as he also stood and began to clear his plates and utensils.

"Thank you, Richard, but it really isn't necessary."

"Hey, I'm good at it living alone as I do. I've learned early on it's not very smart to let dirty dishes build up."

"How do you like living alone?"

"I'm used to it since it's been over seven years since Rachel passed. How about you?"

"I love being alone, although I always enjoy it when Patricia and the family visit. You realize, Richard, that life is a series of changes."

"Yes, I know."

"I believe my life is about to take a change, for the better, I'm sure."

"What do you mean, Anita?"

She stopped, placed the dishes in her hand on the counter, and turned to him.

"I'm not sure if you realize it yet, Richard, but you're going to marry me, and we're going to spend the rest of our lives together."

Richard didn't respond immediately but looked at her. She was sincere and not joking. She smiled at him and looked at him with those dark brown eyes that seemed to tell him she was positively certain of what she had told him.

"I know you probably think that I take a lot for granted, Richard. But I know in my heart, beyond any doubt, that I will fall in love with you and you will also fall in love with me. I'm not so egotistical to think I can know the future for certain, but my woman's intuition makes me positive that we will spend the rest of our lives together as husband and wife."

His first impulse was to laugh at her remark and say something humorous. But looking at her, he was filled with a feeling of loneliness and longing—for Catherine, for Rachel, for his wife, whom he could cling to when he needed to, and he needed to more than ever now. He simply said, "I hope you're right, Anita. I hope you're right."

Her eyes softened, and she approached. She put her arms around him and drew him close to her and kissed him.

"Help me finish cleaning up the kitchen. Then you must go."

"Why?"

"You'll understand later."

CHAPTER SIXTEEN

TREPIDATION

Richard drove the truck into the driveway. He did not enter the garage or exit. He was not sure if he would stay or leave. He had an impulse for another errand similar to the one he had just completed. He had visited Rachel's grave in the Evergreen Cemetery near downtown. They owned two plots together in the Jewish section. He had initially wanted to lay a bouquet of forget-me-nots next to her tombstone. He had decided instead to honor her preference of Jewish tradition and placed a simple but symmetrical small stone on her tombstone in accordance with ancient custom. Knowing Rachel, she would have smiled and understood his expression of love and longing that the flowers would have meant. But he reasoned she would have preferred the simple laying of the stone. It wasn't just any stone. It was a granite stone worn smooth by the running waters of a mountain stream that they had visited in the White Mountains in Eastern Arizona. She had taken several of the small and smooth, rounded stones to place in a small waterfall that she kept on a credenza in the living room.

"Whenever I see these beautiful stones, I will always remember our visit to this wonderful forest. When we are old and gray, seeing and holding these stones again will take us back to our youth," she had told him on the summer day so long ago.

Although he didn't visit her grave on a frequent basis, he did so whenever he was feeling lonely and especially when facing a problem, the solution for which he had not mastered. He had spent a quiet twenty minutes there until a young family came to pay their respects at the grave of the grandmother not too distant from Rachel's.

Rachel, if only we had been able to grow old together. I leave this stone with you. I know that today we are both sharing some pleasure in the memories it brings.

He had intended to drive home but decided to drive to East Lawn Cemetery on Grant Road to visit Jane's grave. He drove out of the driveway toward East Lawn. He stopped at a florist along the way and purchased a bouquet of forget-me-nots. He laid the flowers at the base of Jane's tombstone and stood silently for several minutes, remembering her laughter as they danced that night that seemed so long ago.

He entered his home after checking the empty mailbox. There was no one home. Michael and Shura would be arriving next week from Colorado. It would be nice to have them here again. He poured himself a glass of ice tea and sat in the recliner. His thoughts immediately wandered to Anita and the dinner they had shared five days ago.

When she had spoken of resistance, he had felt a sinking feeling in his heart. Richard did not often think about that fateful night when he and Deidra Gonzalez had killed the two rogue Border Patrol officers. Their attempt to kill his wife, Rachel, had been driven by a deep-seated hatred of what they considered to be people of an inferior race. He did not think of it often because it disturbed something deep in his soul, something he wished was forever in his past, something he knew in his heart that he might have to face again. Was Anita illogically afraid of something that would probably never happen in these United States of America? He wished that were so; he believed that it was so. Still, it was impossible to even causally listen to the news of the nation without realizing that the number of hate crimes and groups were increasing. He thought it likely that the billionaire business man running for president was merely using the political technique that past candidates had used to play *the race card*; it was an unabashed effort to obtain large numbers of supporters who believed that their concept of a white United States was being forever changed by the evolving demographic change. Nixon was the first to do so, and all the Republican presidents since have attempted to emulate him. He decided that the chances of such a race baiting government were not realistic, and he would maintain his focus on completing his work. One of his goals was to try to determine if the catastrophic events of human prehistory was the source of deep-seated conflict in the collective unconscious, and if so, perhaps we could begin to realistically look for a cure to hatred and crime in the human race. He would not dismiss her fears or her resistance, but he would not let it diminish his need to concentrate on completing his work.

He sipped his glass and returned it to the table next to the recliner. He smiled as he recalled her words that they would fall in love with each other and spend the rest of their days together as husband and wife. The thought was pleasant. He wished that it would become true. He arose and went into his study to work on his book.

He had laid out an argument that Velikovsky's work about the catastrophic changes in the solar system had indeed laid the basic mental images in humankind that served as the later impetus for religion, astrology, and astronomy. Over the course of history, humans had since developed the two beliefs and scientific discipline into complex theology and complex systematic discovery and hypotheses. However, all were based on assumptions about the ancient experience of humankind, assumptions that may have not been correct or true. Recent discoveries in epigenetics had led to further understanding of the environmental influence on gene expression without modifying the genetic code. This, he believed, would further shed light on the origin of Jung's archetypes. What he had not been able to understand, nor had he really expected that he would, was how this could help reduce the natural proclivity for conflict and war, which occurred throughout history and which still occurs today. He would be satisfied if his work would help others understand the basis for war, conflict, hatred, and genocide. Hopefully, this understanding would lead others to seek solutions. He was not optimistic. Anita had spoken of the German Enlightenment, which had brought that society into such a higher achievement of social intercourse. Yet despite that, it was followed by the Nazis in the twentieth century. Was humankind doomed to eternal conflict, hatred, and genocide? He recalled the Greek myth of Sisyphus, who was condemned to repeat forever the same meaningless task of pushing a boulder up a mountain, only to see it roll down again.

Would he even achieve a better understanding in his personal life when he had completed his work? He envied the prophets who had been struck with such passion by God, like the one in Pushkin's poem that had achieved such enlightenment and purpose. He knew in his heart that there would be no lightning and thunder or a life-changing understanding for him. He was not disappointed. He was essentially through with his work, and there had been no soul-searing awakening for him. He realized that his path lay in living as best he could and attempt to achieve communication with the universal consciousness that he hoped would, in Jesus's words, help him find that the kingdom of heaven was within him. He would print a final draft as soon as he could get it ready.

CHAPTER SEVENTEEN

LOSS

"I'm glad you chose to show me the White Mountains via the Coronado Trail. It was beautiful. Please let's not take this route again. Thank God, we're back on the flat, if barren, desert again," Shura said as she looked toward Michael, who was driving.

"I thought you'd enjoy it," Michael answered. "Why don't you want to travel US 191 again?"

"Because some of those curves and drop-offs to those very steep canyons below are a little too intimidating, especially if you tend to drive as fast as you do!"

"I never drove faster than the speed limit or thirty-five miles an hour, Shura. You've never expressed anxiety about my driving before. Why now?"

"You were doing thirty-five miles an hour? I saw signs of some ice on the road, and all I could think of was us sliding off the road into one of those canyons. I'm sorry if that upsets you."

Michael laughed. "Shura, I couldn't be upset with you even if I tried! I promise I'll drive no faster than the speed limit or whatever is prudent in your opinion."

"I know, darling. I'm a little out of sync. We've had such a wonderful honeymoon, and I was thinking about my chances of getting pregnant, and I don't want to do anything that would jeopardize our baby. It's just that the mountain roads in Colorado were so much better than this US 191. I never really realized how sparsely populated and empty large parts of Arizona are."

Michael felt a surge of joy at her words. The thoughts of them having a baby were exhilarating to him. He could not help smiling at her and asked, "Do you think you might be pregnant?"

"It's much too early to even worry about it realistically," she answered. "If I'm not, it's not because we haven't been trying. Michael, what is that up ahead?"

He looked ahead of them and saw what appeared to be a trailer and tractor about a mile away. As they approached the area, they could see a green-and-white Border Patrol truck with flashing lights parked to the side of the road behind the large trailer. There was an officer in the middle of the road, signaling to them to stop and pull over. Michael did so, stopping behind the Border Patrol vehicle. He rolled down the window as the officer approached.

"Good afternoon, sir. Do you have any water I could have for these people? We pulled over this tractor trailer on suspicion of illegal drugs and found thirty-two people jammed in there with no water, food, or air-conditioning. We radioed in for a helicopter and additional medical assistance, but the ETA is almost an hour away, and some of them are pretty dehydrated."

"We have two gallons in the ice chest in the trunk. You're welcome to have those," Michael replied as he noticed a man who was obviously the driver sitting on the side of the road in handcuffs.

"Thank you."

The officer opened the door so Michael could exit and open the trunk. Shura also exited and looked at the people sitting on the side of the road. There were no trees or growth to provide shade other than scrub brush. She shaded her eyes with her hand and looked toward several women with children sitting apart from the men.

One woman, nearest to her with a baby in her arms, looked at her and spoke.

"¿Señora, puede ayudarme por favor? Mi bebé tiene mucho calor y sed y me temo que no está bien. ¿Puedo por favor tomar un poco de agua?" Ma'am, can you please help me? My baby is very hot and thirsty, and I'm afraid he is not doing well. Can I please have some water?

"Si, señora. Tengo un poco conmigo en esta botella de agua. Ya voy." Yes, ma'am. I have a little with me in this water bottle. I'm coming.

"Halt! Stop where you are! Do not approach the prisoners!"

Shura had not seen the second officer positioned in front of the men armed with a shotgun who was now screaming at her. She continued to walk toward the woman. As she approached closer, she could see the woman was in physical distress and the baby was comatose. Visions of dying and tortured women and children in the Iraqi desert, prisoners released from ISIS fighters to be used as human shields, appeared before her as if part of the group. She ignored the officer's command and continued to slowly approach the woman.

"Sir, I am an army-trained medic! This woman and child are in extreme distress and need immediate help!" she shouted as she continued to approach the woman and child.

"Stop where you are, or I will shoot you!" the officer commanded, pointing his shotgun toward Shura.

"Stop! Hold your fire!" Michael barked as he sprinted toward Shura. "I'll stop her!"

He was closely followed by the first officer, who drew his weapon and ordered Michael to stop.

"Cease and desist! You're both under arrest for interfering in a lawful arrest of illegal aliens."

Michael stopped in his tracks, fearful for Shura's safety. The officer pursued him and overtook him. He quickly approached Shura with his pistol pointed at her and attempted to knock her down. Instinctively, she parried his blow with one hand, dropped the water bottle, and felled the officer with a blow to his neck.

The second officer with the shotgun fired, striking Shura in the face and chest, knocking her to the ground. Michael rushed to her side to take her into his arms. When he reached her side and knelt beside her, the officer fired again. Although the blast mostly missed him, he immediately felt pain as some of the pellets struck him in the left side and shoulder, knocking him backward.

"Shura, Shura . . .," he cried as he held her in his arms.

CHAPTER EIGHTEEN

REVELATION

Richard was at Anita's house to meet Cassandra Purvis. Cassandra was a member of Anita's group of women who were in the resistance group she founded. Anita had called Richard yesterday to explain that Cassandra wanted to meet him. Her reason was compelling.

Cassandra, Anita had told him, was the only woman in the group who was a pagan. She was not only a pagan but also a practicing one who had her own circle of followers that congregated frequently to participate in rituals.

"She is adamant that she meet you. Angie had lunch with her and two other women at the Mountain Market on Fifth Street. Angie is just an acquaintance of Cassandra, not a close friend. She mentioned you in the course of their discussion and told the group that you were working on a book that sought to index interdisciplinary knowledge in an attempt to determine the origin of religion. No one else seemed to think much of it but Cassandra. She appeared to Angie to act as if she was struck by something that utterly fascinated her. She implored Angie to introduce you to her. When Angie mentioned that you and she were only very casual acquaintances but that I was more familiar with you, she prevailed on Angie for me to introduce the two of you. Hence, I'm on the phone, asking if you could meet her at my house."

"She sounds interesting. I would love to meet her. Is anyone else in her circle part of your resistance?"

"No. She is a wonderful woman if a little off the beaten track in her religious beliefs, but she is perfectly normal in every other way. She was abused by her husband, and after they divorced, she has never married again. She is dedicated to the resistance and never fails to volunteer for any task she is asked to do. She is almost ten years younger than you and attractive, so don't let her cast any of her spells on you."

"What?" Richard asked.

"I'm kidding. You haven't forgotten what I told you the other day, have you?"

"You mean about us falling in love with each other, getting married, and spending the rest of our lives together? Absolutely not. I'm going to work as hard as possible to make it happen."

"And if it doesn't?" she asked.

"Así es la vida, no? C'est la vie," he replied.

"Don't be so easily swayed, oh ye of little faith."

The doorbell rang, and Anita greeted Cassandra, "Come in, Cassandra, and meet Richard Valencia. Richard, this is a friend of mine, Cassandra Purvis."

Cassandra was a little taller than Anita and a little thinner. She had beautiful chestnut brown hair parted on one side, which fell to shoulder length. He noticed a small scattering of gray hair, which only accentuated her pretty face. She wore almost no makeup, but her expressive blue eyes seemed to express a warmth and goodwill as she looked at him. She wore a black A-line dress with white polka dots that fell below her knees.

"Please, everyone, come into the living room. I have prepared a pot of hot water for tea and some light cookies. I know Cassandra enjoys hot tea and cookies during the day. Richard, is this OK, or can I get you something else?" Anita said as she led them into the living room.

"No, thank you, Anita. This is fine," he replied.

"It is so nice to meet you, Richard. I've heard some fascinating stories about you. And that is why I've been so insistent on meeting you," Cassandra said after they were seated.

"I've been looking forward to meeting you as well. I have also heard some fascinating things about you," Richard replied.

"Oh, do you mean about me being a Wiccan? There is not much to get excited about. Those in my coven know me as a high priestess, but in all other respects, I'm a normal woman with normal concerns. But it is not me I want to talk to you about."

She waited expectantly for Richard to respond.

"What is it you want to talk to me about?" Richard asked, becoming more curious at this interesting woman. *Anita is correct,* he thought. *She is very attractive.*

"Angie told me that you have been learning Hebrew. She told me you desire to read the original documents in your research. If you have done so, you may or may not know that the early Hebrews were influenced in their religion, even more, conversed with God with the help of *kaneh-bosm*. Have you heard of it?"

"No. I don't remember coming across that term," he replied, growing more curious.

"*Kaneh-bosm* is a psychoactive drug used by many ancient peoples, including our own pagans, but more importantly, for your work by the ancient Hebrews. Read Exodus 30: 22–23. In that section, you will read about God's instruction to Moses on how to prepare the Tent of the Meeting or the Tent of the Tabernacle and how to infuse it with anointing oil. The anointing oil is similar to cannabis. There are many references in the Old Testament to it and how to use it. This is the incense that the Hebrew women burned to the Queen of Heaven in the high places so often mentioned in that document. The Queen of Heaven in the Old Testament is Yahweh's consort. Her name is Asherah. She is also our goddess. Many of my people call her the Moon Goddess, but in reality, she is the planet Venus. The point I want to make is that you can't understand the origin of religion without considering the effect of psychoactive drugs used by the Hebrews and other ancient peoples."

"That's interesting," Richard said. "Velikovsky documented that not only the Queen of Heaven was the planet Venus but also many other female deities in the ancient world. Have you read Velikovsky's works?"

"No, but I will. My sources are ancient texts that pagans have used for at least a thousand years. They incorporate the knowledge, wisdom, and beliefs of such people as the Druids, those who have long believed in and practiced witchcraft as well as the Wiccans."

"Thanks. I will add some of those references to my study."

"One more point," Cassandra said. "Have you ever heard about a psychiatrist named Julian Jaynes?"

"Yes! As a matter of fact, I reference him in my work! One of his theses is that consciousness, as he defines it, introspection, only came about with the development of language. It is a very cogent theory and one that has certainly not been disproven, although not currently as popular as it once was. It is becoming more prevalent with those working in the field of consciousness."

"Then you agree that ancient man was not as fully conscious as modern man. According to Jaynes, ancient humans were not able to introspect, so they may have experienced their higher thinking, or cognitive functioning, as auditory hallucinations or what they believed were the voices of God or the gods. Am I on the correct track?" she asked.

"Yes, but please realize that I have done no original work in this area. I've only read Jaynes's works and believe his observations may play a part in the origin of religion."

"Well, I believe that Jaynes was on the right track, but he failed to realize or understand the importance the psychoactive drugs played in those hallucinations, which man's right brain communicated to his left brain as the voices of God. By the way, I accept his theory, but without language, how could the right brain communicate with the left brain? I certainly don't know the answer or even if it's a realistic question, but it is puzzling to me."

"Cassandra, you asked an excellent question. It is also one that I cannot answer. I'm not dodging your question, but please realize that I'm only compiling work of others whose effort may help us discover the origin of religion. If Jaynes provided a technical answer to that question, which he well may have, I don't know it."

"When Genesis describes God's commandments on how to anoint the Tent of the Meeting with oil, the Hebrews were following an even more ancient tradition of ancient peoples, including the Scythians." Cassandra continued. "Archeologists have discovered that the Scythians would construct tents in which to burn cannabis-like substance on the steppes when there were no caves available to do so. They then would position their heads into the tents to inhale the smoke of the burning cannabis and, in doing so, would consecrate the act to their goddess Tabiti. Tabiti is their Moon Goddess, similar to ours, and is the Queen of Heaven."

Richard's cell phone began to ring.

"Excuse me, please. I have to take this. The caller ID indicates it is from the Department of Public Safety."

The two women could hear him say hello as he walked out the front door onto the porch. They both watched closely at his movements as he listened on the phone and then spoke briefly. When he returned into the living room, he was ashen.

"Richard, please tell me. What has happened?" Anita implored.

"That was a sergeant from the Arizona Department of Public Safety. He wanted to know where I was and is driving right now to give me some news about my son, Michael, and daughter-in-law, Shura. Something happened on the highway in Graham County, and he needs to inform me in person."

"What should we do?" Anita asked.

"I was told to wait at this address until Sergeant Westover arrives with the information."

"How did they locate you?" Anita asked.

"Apparently from either Michael's or Shura's cell phones. They also ran Michael's driver's license information in their computer system and found his address to be my home. I was listed in Michael's and Shura's cell phones as Dad, so when they cross-referenced the phone numbers with our address, they knew who I was."

"Maybe it's not too serious," Cassandra volunteered.

"I'm afraid it's very bad for them to find me and send a sergeant to inform me personally," Richard replied with his head down.

Fifteen minutes later, an Arizona Highway Patrol car with the words "State Trooper" emblazoned on the side pulled up and parked in front of the house. All three watched as the officer exited and walked to the front door.

As the sergeant approached the porch, Anita opened the door and greeted him, "Hello, Sergeant. I'm Anita Castellano, and this is my house. Richard Valencia is a friend of mine and is waiting for you in the living room. Please come in. My friend Cassandra and I will go to another room to give you privacy."

"Thank you, ma'am. I'm Sgt. Riley Westover. I do need to talk to Mr. Valencia alone."

Richard stood and greeted the sergeant, "Sir, I am very sorry to deliver this sad news about your son, Michael, and his wife, Shura Valencia. They were involved in an incident involving Border Patrol and a tractor trailer filled with illegal immigrants on the US 191 Highway in Graham County about thirty miles south of Safford. These are the facts as I know them from one of two Border Patrol agents involved in the encounter. The Border Patrol is conducting an investigation, and you will be notified by the Arizona Highway Patrol as soon as our part of the investigation is complete. There will be a reference to the Border

Patrol investigation that will assist you in obtaining a copy of their report.

"Two Border Patrol officers on routine patrol observed a suspicious tractor trailer driving north on US 191. Apparently, the combination took a circuitous route to avoid driving through Willcox, which would have been the most expeditious route and which most travelers from the south of Safford driving north would normally take. The two officers believed that there was a high probability that the rig was carrying illegal drugs and decided to make a traffic stop after they trailed the vehicle and observed several mud flaps missing, which gave them probable cause to effect the stop. Once they were out of their car and talking to the driver, they heard pounding coming from the inside of the trailer. They placed the driver under arrest and made him open the trailer, which was secured by several locks. When they opened the trailer doors, they found what were thirty-two illegal immigrants packed inside without food, water, or air-conditioning. Some of the people were in fairly bad shape. The officers had them exit the trailer and sit on the side of the road. The men were separated from the women and children and under armed guard by one of the officers armed with a service-issued shotgun as well as his service pistol.

"Apparently, not very long after they had secured the driver and immigrants, your son and daughter-in-law approached them from the north in their SUV. One of the officers flagged them down and asked if they had any water they could share with the immigrants, some of whom were severely dehydrated. Your son readily agreed and opened the trunk and provided two gallons of water to the officer. In the interim, your daughter-in-law had also exited the vehicle with a small container of water. One of the women immigrants with a baby was closest to her and asked her in Spanish to help her and her baby, who was dying in her arms and who passed shortly after the incident. Apparently, your daughter-in-law spoke Spanish and told the woman she would help her and walked toward her. The armed Border Patrol officer ordered her to stop and not approach the immigrants. She responded to the officer that she was an army-trained medic and that the woman and baby were in severe distress and she needed to assist them. She disobeyed the officer's orders to stop. When she continued to approach the immigrants, he again warned her and told her he would shoot her if she continued.

"At this time, your son ran toward his wife, yelling for her to stop. The second officer dropped the water and drew his weapon and ran after your son, ordering him to stop. Your son obeyed the officer. The officer then continued on to your daughter-in-law's location with his weapon pointed at her. Apparently, he was trying to handcuff her and take her into custody. He approached too close, and she knocked the weapon out of his hand, and with her other, she delivered a blow to his throat, which rendered him unable to breathe normally, and he went into shock. It was at this time that the second officer fired his shotgun at her, gravely injuring her. Your son ran to her side, and as he took her into his arms, the officer fired his shotgun at your son, wounding him on the left side of his body, but he stayed with your daughter-in-law until medical assistance arrived about thirty minutes later. Backup provided by the Highway Patrol and medical assistance arrived on the scene and secured it. The Highway Patrol sent a medevac helicopter to airlift your son and daughter-in-law to the trauma center at Our Mother of Sorrows hospital in Phoenix. I have the information here on this card for you to contact the hospital to inquire on their status."

"Is Michael under arrest?" Richard asked.

"Not by the Highway Patrol. I believed the Border Patrol intends to place them both under arrest when they are discharged from the hospital. I believe they will be charged with interfering in a lawful law enforcement action."

Richard looked the young sergeant in the eyes and asked, "What exactly did Shura and Michael do that was so bad? I know Shura. She was truly trying to help that woman and child. That was no crime. Also, I can understand why Michael would run to her side. They were newlywed and returning from their honeymoon in Colorado. What is the crime in rushing to your wounded bride's side?"

"From what I can tell, sir, there was no crime. The Border Patrol is expanding so rapidly that not only is the quality of their recruits not what it should be, but they also do not receive the same level of training as the Highway Patrol. I believe that our state troopers would have been able to handle the same situation without injury to anyone. That's all I can say at this point. Do you have any questions, sir?"

"No. Who can I call at the Highway Patrol if I do?"

"Our number is on the card, along with my name, rank, and a department-issued case number to which you can refer when you speak to someone."

"Thank you. I'll be leaving for Phoenix and Our Mother of Sorrows hospital immediately."

"Drive carefully, sir. Good luck."

Richard walked the sergeant to the door and watched him until he drove out of sight.

The two women were behind him.

"Richard, that is terrible news," Anita said. "Are you sure you want to leave immediately for Phoenix?"

"Yes. I'm not even going home. I'll worry about details later. Right now, I have to go to my son."

"Then I will go with you, Richard," Anita said. "Wait here just a minute while I grab some water bottles and a change of clothes for myself. I won't be more than a minute. I do not want you driving alone."

When they were alone, Cassandra approached him and spoke.

"Richard, I know that this is not the time to discuss this, but when things have settled down, please come see me. I have erected a tent in my backyard, and I want you to experience what the ancient Hebrews experienced in the Tent of the Ark when they conversed with God. Don't say anything now. You have a full plate. I will pray for you. Good luck."

During the drive to Phoenix, Richard placed an international call to Naomi Sverdlov. He was fortunate that she was home and able to take the call. After he explained what few details he had about Michael and Shura, she expressed her great concern and asked what she could do.

"Naomi, you are well known and respected in Israel. Can I ask you to contact people you know who may have influence on providing some pressure on United States authorities to intercede on Shura's behalf? She was only attempting to provide aid to an immigrant woman whose child was dying when she was shot. She is not only an Israel citizen but also a soldier whom I know served with distinction in the armed forces. Michael has told me that she became well known in Israel through the media with stories of her joining the Peshmerga against the government's wishes."

"Yes, I will, Richard. I also know Mustafa Qadir, who was and is a high-ranking government official associated with the PUK. I met him during fieldwork in a Tell, which uncovered a Babylonian library. He not only provided security for my team and me, but we also became fast friends. I have done several favors for him when he needed someone to run interference in Israeli politics. I have visited him several times since my work there, and he has always been a graceful and gracious host. I have read several articles about Shura in Israeli newspapers. Technically, she violated Israeli law by entering Iraq and fighting with the Peshmerga, but she is considered a heroine by many here. I will do my best."

"Thank you, Naomi. I will be forever indebted to you for anything you can do," Richard said.

"It is my pleasure. By the way, have you given any consideration to my offer to join me here in Israel? I am certain we would make a good team. My door, as well as my heart, is always open to you."

"I will never forget your offer, Naomi. I will keep in touch with you. Right now, I must focus on Michael and Shura."

"I truly understand, Richard. *Hashem yevarech otha.* Shalom." (God be with you.)

Richard replied as he terminated the call, *"Shalom aleikhem,* Naomi. Thank you." (Peace be unto you.)

It was several minutes before Anita spoke.

"I know now is not the time, Richard, to ask you who that woman is and how you know her. If and when circumstances permit, I will ask you."

"Thank you, Anita. And thank you for coming with me. You are a comfort to me."

By the time they arrived at the hospital and parked, they were advised at the emergency room that Shura had just completed surgery in the trauma center and was in a recovery room with Michael at her side. Appending the authorized visitor passes to their clothing and following instructions, they arrived on the second floor and pressed the buzzer at the entrance door.

"May I help you?" the woman's voice asked on the intercom.

"I'm Richard Valencia, Michael Valencia's father and Shura Valencia's father-in-law. I'm here with a good friend to visit them."

"Please come in and sign in at the desk."

After they had signed in, they were directed to room 264, which was down a long hallway just prior to an exit door. There was an armed young Border Patrol officer sitting outside the door. He stood and greeted them as they approached, "Good evening, Mr. Valencia. I'm Agent Jeffrey Watts. I'm posted here strictly as a precaution because Border Patrol regulations call for an agent to be available in circumstances like this. If you need anything, please do not hesitate to ask me."

"Thank you, Agent Watts. Can you tell me if my son and his wife are under arrest by the Border Patrol?"

"No, sir. I believe from instructions from my superior that they are considered persons of interest in a pending investigation, and I'm here as much for their protection as to ensure they will be available when released from the hospital."

"Thank you for that information. Can we go in now?"

"Yes, sir," Agent Watts replied, holding the door open for them.

Michael stood and embraced his father.

"Dad, thanks for coming. Are you OK?" he asked.

Richard noticed his left forearm was in a bandage and he had dried bloodstains on his shirt.

"Michael, you've been hurt. Are you OK?"

"Yes, I am, Dad. I have some superficial wounds from the shotgun pellets, but I was fortunate that the main grouping missed me. I've lost a little blood but nothing to be concerned over. What about you? Are you OK?"

"I'm fine. This is my good friend Anita Castellano. I happened to have been visiting with her at her home when the Highway Patrol contacted me. A sergeant, Riley Westover, came by her house and personally told me what had happened. I have the information with me if you need it later. How is Shura?"

Michael smiled at Anita. "I'm very pleased to meet you, ma'am. Please have a seat. Can I get you some water or juice?"

"It is my pleasure to meet you as well, Michael. Please, how is Shura? Your father has been on pins and needles on the trip up here, worrying about her."

All three looked at Shura as she lay sleeping under sedation. There were several sensors attached to her right wrist, and an intravenous tube was attached to a plastic container filled with fluid on a metal stand next to her bed. Her left arm was heavily bandaged and in a sling, held in position across her midsection. The top of her head was wrapped in bandages and so was the left side of her face. There was a bandage next to her left eye.

"Fortunately, she will recover, although she will need some plastic surgery on the left side of her face. Several pellets struck her there and had to be surgically removed. Thank God, they narrowly missed her eye. The main blast of pellets struck her arm, breaking it in two places, below and above the elbow. She was operated on to reset it and will receive a cast on it in the next few days. I've been told that she will need physical therapy to regain full use of her left arm. Come and sit down. It's been a long day for all of us."

"Michael, during our trip from Tucson, I called a very good friend of mine in Israel by the name of Naomi Sverdlov. Maybe you remember me telling you something about her."

"Yes, I do. She is a scholar of ancient writing and well known for her work, is that not correct?"

"Yes. She is not only known but also widely respected in Israel and has some friends in position of authority. I have requested her to ask someone with authority to intercede in Shura's behalf. From the English translations of the newspaper articles about Shura you sent me, apparently, she is regarded as somewhat of a heroine and well liked there."

"Thanks, Dad. This whole thing didn't have to happen. It was a terrible misunderstanding on the part of the two Border Patrol agents. That is not only my opinion. Earlier, I was visited by a high-ranking Border Patrol agent, Phillip Greaves, who has been assigned to investigate this incident and who has over twenty years of service and was a former district commander in the Tucson sector. He asked me if I was related to you. He remembers your incident with Mom and Diedra Gonzalez and highly respects you for what you did. He also told me that the chief of the Border Patrol received a call from the director of Homeland Security, advising him that the Israeli ambassador had made a formal request into the incident involving one of their citizens. After talking to him, he informed me that the Border Patrol has placed the incident agent's arrest of Shura and me on hold. We are officially designated as persons of interest, witnesses to an incident involving prisoners and shots fired. I also called Lieutenant Colonel Kensington, who was my boss in Iraq, then a major but recently promoted, and related in detail what happened. I asked him for any assistance he could give me, and he was pretty strong in his assurance that he would do everything he could to make sure the chain of command was aware of what happened. That's about all I know at this point, although I intend to do some serious follow-up in the morning. By the way, where are you staying tonight?"

"Don't worry about us, Michael. We'll find a hotel nearby and get some rest. Are you staying here with Shura tonight?"

"Yes. I won't leave until we leave together."

After two hours with Michael and Shura, who remained sleeping quietly under sedation, Richard hugged his son and left the hospital with Anita. They managed to locate a hotel about two miles from the hospital. After they had parked the car, he turned to her and asked, "Do I get one room or two?"

"One room, Richard, with two beds if you like. I'm fine with just one queen-size bed."

After they were in the room and preparing for bed, he paused and looked at her.

"I left in such a rush that I don't have any pajamas. I'll have to sleep in my shorts."

"Don't worry about it. I brought not only a change of clothes but also a nightgown. I also brought you a new toothbrush if you want."

"You're very thoughtful, Anita. Thank you."

"It's what every wife would do for her husband, not that we're married yet." She smiled as she went into the bathroom to change and brush her teeth.

When Richard was through in the bathroom and entered, she was already in bed, sitting up in her nightgown and looking at him with a smile. He stripped down to his shorts and hung his clothes in the closet. He could feel her eyes as she watched him closely.

"A penny for your thoughts," he said.

"You look pretty good for your age, Richard. You must work at keeping fit."

"Does that mean you like what you see?" he asked as he slipped under the covers.

"It means I like everything about you. Hold me close," she said as she cuddled next to him. "Not tonight, Richard. Just hold me close. We have the rest of our lives. *Si Dios quiere y el arroyo no se levanta*." (God willing and the creek don't rise.)

CHAPTER NINETEEN

THE QUEEN OF HEAVEN

Richard placed the newspaper on the kitchen counter and walked into the living room with his cup of coffee in his hand to answer the phone.

"Hello, this is Richard," he greeted.

"Richard, this is Naomi. It's been five days since you called me on your trip to Phoenix. How are Michael and Shura?"

"Naomi, it's great to hear from you. Michael was not seriously wounded, thank God. Shura received the brunt of a blast from a shotgun, which broke her left arm in two places and embedded several pellets in the left side of her face. She will be released from the hospital today, and she and Michael will drive to Tucson. She will undergo some plastic surgery here in Tucson. They're living with me in the guesthouse. I want to thank you for your assistance. By the time I arrived at the hospital, I was informed by Michael that a senior Border Patrol officer informed him that the Israeli ambassador had formally requested information on Shura as an Israeli citizen. I believe that is the reason that the chief of the Border Patrol suspended their arrest and they are now considered persons of interest."

"You're welcome, Richard. I was glad that I was able to help in a small way. I happen to know the prime minister as well as his chief of staff. I called the chief and asked him to repay a favor he owed me, and he was most willing to do so. I also called Mustafa Qadir and asked him to use his influence with the Iraqi prime minister in requesting information on Shura through the American ambassador in Baghdad. That may be a little more difficult because there is some tension between the Kurds and the Iraqi government over their autonomous region and current occupation of some very rich oil fields. But we shall see. Is Michael fit to drive?"

"Yes. The Border Patrol impounded his SUV and had one of their contract towing services tow it. They impounded it in their yard in Willcox. With the help of a senior Border Patrol agent, the vehicle was released to me, and I dropped it off at the hospital on the way home. Fortunately, I had a friend with me to drive my vehicle from Willcox to Phoenix."

"I am glad to hear Michael and Shura will be OK. It was quite a shock to them, I'm sure. After all they have experienced with their military service, it just doesn't seem right that something like this should happen. I don't want to get involved in politics, Richard, but I see some troublesome events happening in America, which remind me of the early thirties in Germany. But I will let you go for now. Remember my offer to you. Shalom."

"Shalom, Naomi. I will be forever grateful to you."

Richard returned the phone to its cradle and sat in the recliner with his coffee in hand. He had finished preparations for Michael and Shura's return. He arranged for a housecleaning and maid service to clean the guesthouse, and he had stocked it with the things they would need. He had gone grocery shopping, and the kitchen was also well stocked with food and drink.

He took a sip of coffee and then sat back to think. His thoughts turned to what Cassandra Purvis had told him about the ancient Hebrews and their use of the psychoactive drug *kaneh-bosm*. He had never used any substance stronger than alcohol, and he drank only occasionally. He had never desired to experiment with any drug nor had he ever intended to do so. However, Cassandra's information about the ancient's use of psychoactive drugs, including cannabis, in a religious context fascinated him. He remembered reading about the mystery surrounding the Ark of the Covenant in Velikovsky's *Worlds in Collision* and considered it a distinct possibility that Cassandra was correct. This view was confirmed by his research on the Internet. He had made up his mind to take her up on her offer to experience her tent to better understand the experience. He would not tell Anita about it until it was over.

It is time to call Cassandra, Richard thought. *It is time to burn incense to the Queen of Heaven.*

Richard skipped lunch and had an early light meal for dinner before picking up the telephone and calling Cassandra.

"Hello," she greeted.

"Cassandra, this is Richard Valencia. I've been thinking of your offer to more intimately experience the effects of *kaneh-bosm*. I've done a little research, including the Old Testament references in Exodus. I've had a somewhat long day and am a little tired. I understand from my research that some of the ancients would enter the Tent of the Meeting and the pillar of smoke from the sacrificial cannabis. They would relax, allowing them to sleep, during which they would experience a dream oracle. Am I on track?"

"Precisely. I've been expecting your call. I have a large camping tent semi-permanently set up in my backyard, and I've prepared the mixture as closely as I can to the description in Genesis. When would you like to experience it? If you are a little tired, this evening might be a good time."

"Thank you. I am eager to experience this to better understand your observations and theory about communicating with God. Is this evening OK with you?"

"Yes. I'm free tonight. I live in a mobile home on two acres off of Old Spanish Trail about thirteen miles east from where it intersects with Houghton Road. When can you arrive? Sunset is about five forty or so."

"If I leave now, I can be there in forty-five minutes. Can you text me your address and I'll enter it into my truck's GPS?"

"I will. I'll hang up now and text you. I'll see you soon. Bye."

"Goodbye, Cassandra. Thanks."

It was almost sunset when Richard arrived at the closed gate to Cassandra's property. He exited the truck, opened the unlocked gate, drove through, and reclosed it, arriving at the modern double-wide manufactured home two minutes later. She opened the door as he parked next to the house.

"Good evening," she greeted him with a smile. "Come inside, and I will explain how this will go tonight."

Richard followed her into the house and sat on a large stuffed chair in the spacious living room. The room was tastefully furnished with contemporary furniture, several framed paintings, and two large vases of flowers. There was a large picture window facing the yard. Richard noticed a large octagon camping tent. He was looking to the northwest because he could see part of the setting sun over the horizon.

"Can I offer you something to drink, a glass of tea or a soft drink?"

"No, thank you, Cassandra. I am eager to get started."

"Good. Everything is ready. I have a large two-room camping tent set up in my yard. It's large enough to sleep eight people easily. In the middle, I have a wooden table with the material in a large stone plate. I have prepared the incense as closely as possible in accordance with the words in Exodus 30. There is a small opening in the vent in the middle so that the smoke does not get too thick to breathe. There is a padded recliner in one room with a small table next to it. If you should become sleepy, you can nap comfortably in the recliner. I see you brought a notebook. You can place that on the table so if you desire to take notes, it will be available. Do not worry about me or the time. If you should fall asleep, you can sleep until tomorrow morning. I will be awake in the house. You can enter through the back door, which we will pass through to the yard. Do you have any questions?"

"No. This will be a first for me. I've read a little in my research about what I'll feel so I'm as ready as possible."

"Good. Follow me."

He followed her down the back stairs and into the tent. He saw the table with a large round stone plate on top and observed her light a fire. He immediately smelled a fragrance that brought back childhood memories of the priest burning incense during the mass. She directed him to sit in the chair and relax.

"I'll close the flap to the tent with fastener straps so if you need to exit, you can do so easily. There is an opening in the other room similar to the one in this room. It's only partially covered so the room and the tent will remain ventilated. Since the incense burns slowly, you will see a column of smoke rising from it. Some of it will exit through the opening at the top, but there will be enough that will permeate the tent so you should begin to feel the effects in a short period. If you need me, just come on in to the house. I'll be there waiting."

"Thanks. Don't worry about me. I'll be fine."

She lighted the fire and returned to the house. He stood by the table for a few minutes, breathing normally. He could feel the light sensation of smoke as it entered his mouth and nose. He sat in the recliner, placed the notebook and a pen on the table next to it, sat back, took a deep breath, and relaxed. He had learned to practice deep breathing exercises in the navy. He had experienced what a flight surgeon told him was *white coat fright* during his annual physical examinations required by his flight status. During the first couple of exams, his initial blood pressure was higher than acceptable, requiring him to return for five consecutive days for daily measurement. The follow-up checkups were always normal. The flight surgeon explained that he was in good physical condition but was slightly nervous about the physical exam. He then taught him breathing and visualization techniques to lower his blood pressure to acceptable measurements. Richard had successfully learned and applied the techniques and was able to control his blood pressure. He now practiced that technique and slowly felt a pleasant wave of relaxation surge through him. After completing his breathing exercises, he mentally commanded himself to *relax now* knowing that his subconscious would begin to comply and he would slip into self-hypnosis. He extended the recliner, which lifted his feet up and placed him in a near horizontal position and continued his meditation.

Now relaxed and with his eyes closed, he decided to release control of his thoughts and let them flow randomly. He remembered growing up as a youth in a loving and close-knit family. His father was a career navy sailor who retired as a master chief gunner's mate. It was because of the influence of his father that he chose the navy as his career. Unfortunately, that career was cut short by the tragic and untimely death of his wife and young daughter. His memories of that time were mostly pleasant. He remembered meeting and dating Catherine, their love and their marriage. It was soon after that Bernadette was born. She was his beautiful and precocious daughter. When he lost them, he had been devastated and sought solace on a solitary trek through El Camino del Diablo. It was a result of that journey that he unexpectedly met his second love and wife, Rachel. Together, they had two beautiful children, Sarah and Michael.

Richard had been raised a Catholic but had never been pious or observant like his parents. After he met Rachel, he converted to her faith, Judaism, and it was in this faith that they reared their two children. Richard had always been at peace in his new faith, although he did not consider himself pious. He had remained observant under the gentle and loving assistance from Rachel. Deep within his understanding, he realized that he had not yet found the ultimate solace of religion he sought. After Rachel had passed, the idea began to grow within him that human interdisciplinary understanding of the universe was creating a new paradigm from which it may now be possible to discover the origin of religion. He and Rachel had experienced racial hatred in a small number of Border Patrol agents with close ties to white supremacist organizations in Arizona. She had believed in and practiced Tikkun Olam.[23] During her defense of a woman whose husband had been shot and killed by a rogue agent, she had come to the unwelcome attention of those who hated her not only for her actions but also for her Jewishness.

He could not understand what the root of antisemitism was and had begun to study it even before the incident in which he killed two agents. After that, he began to more earnestly seek answers. After Rachel had passed, he had more time to devote to his effort, and that was when he began to formulate his compendium of work by experts in their fields. It was to be the datum from which he sought the origin of religion.

His memories began to flow somewhat similar to a slow reversal of a videotape. He recognized flashes of visions as they cascaded through his awareness. Shutting his eyes tightly, he tried to focus on the image within his mind.

Richard felt a cool and pleasant breeze gently flowing against his face. He looked around to determine where he was. He saw what appeared to be a large outdoor altar set on an elevated platform. In front of the altar, he noticed three priests who appeared to be supplicating themselves and gazing upward into the heavens. They appeared similar to paintings on ancient Egyptian tombs and temples he had seen in museums and textbooks. When he looked toward the direction of the sky to which they were focused, he was shocked and overwhelmed at the breathtaking apparition he witnessed. In the heavens, he beheld a prodigious sight, a stupendous orb in the heavens brightly illuminated against the night sky. Its colossal presence filled the sky from horizon to horizon. Within the behemoth apparition, he saw a brightly illuminated smaller orb from which bright rays emanated in all directions. In the center of this

---

[23] Tikkun Olam is a Jewish concept defined by acts of kindness performed to perfect or repair the world. The phrase is found in the Mishnah, a body of classical rabbinic teachings.

smaller sphere, he witnessed a lesser red globe. There did not appear to be the vast array of stars he expected but a watery mist, which to him appeared to be floating over the earth. From his memories of the creation account in Genesis, he recognized what were described as the waters of chaos. From his recollection of the descriptions in Velikovsky's writings and in *The Saturn Myth*, he realized that he was looking at what to humankind appeared to be the emergence of the first god, the benign creator. *Behold,* he thought, *the emergence of the Lord of Hosts. I am in Egypt, at a holy site in an ancient land.*

He saw clearly and distinctly that what he was looking at had been described by Talbott as the polar configuration. He knew he was looking at the original Holy Trinity. The illuminated orbs in his sight clearly resembled the halos he had observed in religious artwork.

The scene before him began to fade, and the waters of chaos slowly darkened his perception of the vista he had experienced. He closed and opened his eyes to a different but somewhat vaguely familiar image that emerged from the flowing mist.

Judaism is an ancient and holy faith. From what appeared to him to be an emerging scene before him as an observer close to but not a participant, he visualized Moses climbing Mount Sinai to receive God's covenant. He recalled the previous covenants with Abraham and Isaac. He was standing near the gathering of Israelites who remained at the base of Sinai and could feel their fear and foreboding. He heard the thundering rumble and also was struck with great fear of the Lord. He knew fear and anger when he beheld the *golden calf* built by gathering all the gold available from the multitude. Seeing the golden calf raised on its platform and administered to by the Israelites, he clearly perceived and understood Velikovsky's description of the Great Bull of Heaven as the Sun of Night. The planet Saturn appeared in ancient skies as the stupendous prodigy worshipped as the first deity, the Lord of Hosts, and was seen on earth as a massive globe illuminated by a crescent of light reflected by the sun as the configuration of planets locked in phased array rotated on its axis around that orb.

He was aware of this awakening within him somehow entering into his mind's eye.[24] He could smell the fragrance he remembered as incense burned by the priest at evening mass he had attended in his youth. Incense burned to the Queen of Heaven was an ancient rite, one which he now understood the Israelites used in the Tent of the Ark. This knowledge came to him with a clarity and distinctness he had never before experienced.

There is great disorder and chaos. The Levites are killing the men, women, and children of those who had forsaken the Lord of Hosts and built the golden calf. The fierce anger of the Lord could not be averted until the slaughter was done. It was from this day that the Levites from the tribe of Kohath would be sanctified as priests to offer sacrifice. Richard observed from a distance the merciless slaughter of those who had transgressed.

I hear the prophets. I am engulfed with the fear of the Lord of Hosts. He had to shut his eyes at the blinding light of Isaiah. He remembered Velikovsky's words that the light that Isaiah spoke of was caused by the occlusion of Saturn and Jupiter and preceded the flood by seven days. Isaiah had spoken of the coming Messiah.

Isaiah, was he hearing the words of the prophet as he described how the mighty was fallen?

"How you have fallen from heaven, morning star, son of the dawn! You have been cast down to the earth, you who once laid low the nations!"[25]

Isaiah is speaking of Lucifer, the bright morning star, the Queen of Heaven. I am observing an ancient ritual with these Israelites, burning incense to the queen.

---

[24] The mental faculty of conceiving imaginary or recollected scenes, https://www. merriam-webster.com/dictionary/mind's%20eye (accessed January 12, 2018).

[25] Isaiah 14:12.

Suddenly, Richard was walking on a beach on a foreign land. There was a man ahead of him. How he knew the stranger was Augustine of Hippo he did not know, but he was certain. "Augustine, he cried!" The man turned to face him. He appeared to be fifty or sixty years old. He had flowing long brown hair streaked with several white strands. His full white beard had once been dark as indicated by the few strands of dark that sparsely colored his beard that covered his neck. He wore a long garment similar to a multicolored poncho that almost entirely covered an undergarment. Richard noticed the worn thick sandals on his feet.

"Is it true," Richard asked, "that you consider the Trinity one of the most perplexing mysteries of Christianity?"

"Who are you?" Augustine asked. "You are a stranger from a distant shore. Why do you ask?"

"Because I know that the origin of the Holy Trinity lies in the beginning of religion when ancient man looked to the heavens and saw the trinity of Saturn, who many consider the Holy Father, Venus, the Queen of Heaven, and the planet Mars, the son and defender of the faith."

"Blasphemy!" he cried! "Go! Leave my presence! Return to your faraway land so that I may contemplate without distraction!" Richard turned and walked away from the presence of the respected and saintly father of the church.

He was not sure how he had entered a magnificent edifice, but he heard voices in the distance within a structure that was lighted by burning torches on thick stone walls. The voices were speaking in a tongue that to him seemed to be Spanish but with a foreign accent and using some words that he could not understand. It was Spanish; the syntax and words became recognizable to him. He turned from the passage way and entered a chamber that appeared to be the loft of a larger room. He approached a wooden rail about five feet in height and peered over it. Below him, he saw several men dressed in medieval costume sitting around two men who were standing and speaking in turns. From the way the two men addressed each other, he recognized that he was witnessing a conversation between a prelate of the church and a Jewish scholar, Friar Pablo Christiani and Rabbi Nahmanides, the great Rambam. He listened closely as the Rabbi spoke.

> *It seems most strange that . . . the Creator of Heaven and Earth resorted to the womb of a certain Jewish lady, grew there for nine months and was born as an infant, and afterwards grew up and was betrayed into the hands of his enemies who sentenced him to death and executed him, and that afterwards . . . he came to life and returned to his original place. The mind of a Jew, or any other person, simply cannot tolerate these assertions. You have listened all your life to the priests who have filled your brain and the marrow of your bones with this doctrine, and it has settled into you because of that accustomed habit. [I would argue that if you were hearing these ideas for the first time, now, as a grown adult], you would never accept them.[26]*

No! Richard thought. *The Creator of the universe can do as He will regardless if human minds fail to understand his motive! He knew King James would reward Nahmanides three hundred gold pieces for his superlative disputation, although he would be banned from Spain for two years of exile by the church. Why couldn't the rabbi understand that humans can never fully understand the will of the Creator?*

Is Christ the redemption from near annihilation of the world witnessed by men during the capture and reconfiguration of the brown dwarf star from which humankind emerged? Is not

[26] Disputation of Barcelona, *Wikipedia, The Free Encyclopedia,* https://en.wikipedia.org/w/index.php?title=Disputation_of_Barcelona&oldid=813284954 (accessed December 19, 2017).

Kukulkan,²⁷ the first benevolent and loving lawgiver of the Mayans, the hope for redemption? Why did the gods revolt and slay him? Mankind is eternally grateful that Kukulkan's soul rose smoking from his death during the revolt when the sun didn't shine and entered the heavens to become the bright morning dtar? The Mayan calendar tracked the bright morning star's movement through the heavens as attested to by their calendar. Did not Jesus say I am the bright morning star? ²⁸

Richard was becoming confused and losing touch with the images in his mind's eye. *I must leave this tent and go outside to see the heavenly host.*

Richard felt the cool night air and realized he was beginning to emerge from a trancelike euphoria. He did not know how long he had been in the tent or how long he had been standing outside. He knelt on one knee to steady himself. Where had he been? Had he heard the prophets? He vividly remembered the golden calf elevated on a platform at the base of Mount Sinai.

One of the last things he remembered was Shura, beautiful and dressed in flowing white robes, praying with both her arms uplifted. He recognized her words from Isaiah: "Tell me who shall go? Send me Lord. I will go."

"Richard, you've done it. You've experienced the effects of *kaneh-bosm*. Let me help to steady you then come into the house."

Richard looked at the woman who was speaking to him. She was beautiful. Was she an angel sent by the Lord to administer to him? *No, she is Cassandra. She is a witch.*

"Cassandra, what kind of a witch are you? Do you practice black magic? Do you practice white magic? Why do I trust you? You are beautiful."

---

²⁷ Kukulkan, the first god of the Mayans known to the Aztecs and Toltecs as Quetzalcoatl.

²⁸ Revelation 22:16.

"Come, Richard. The effects are beginning to wear off. You will be all right again soon. I will help you into the house and serve you some strong black coffee I've just brewed."

Richard sat at the kitchen table and looked at the beautiful woman, this angel who had come to him in the dark of night to lead him into the warmth and light of this room.

She placed a hot mug of steaming coffee in front of him and then placed her face close to his. He could smell her sweet breath and looked into her beautiful blue eyes. They gazed into each other's eyes. He was captivated by her beauty and her femininity.

"You're coming out of the effects of incense, Richard. Your eyes are still dilated, but I believe you will shortly return to normal."

"Where am I? I don't recognize where I am."

"You are in my home. You don't recognize this room because it's my kitchen, and you entered and exited the house through a different set of doors. Trust me. You will soon be back to normal."

"Cassandra, I am beginning to remember. You are a beautiful witch and a pagan. Am I under your spell?"

She laughed and reached out to touch his cheek.

"No, Richard. I can no more place you under a spell than you can place me under one. Besides, to answer your question, I would be what you called a witch who practices white magic. But that is not a correct description of paganism. I am more a high priestess in a religion. Paganism is as much of a religion as Christianity or Judaism or any other religion. Your quest for the origin of religion pertains as much to mine as it does to yours."

"What time is it?" Richard asked, glancing at his wrist watch.

"It is twelve thirty in the morning," she answered. "You were in the tent for about six hours. I'm not sure how long you were under the effect of the incense. How do you feel?"

"Not quite myself. I am also tired, fatigued, like I've done strenuous work or exercise."

"Come, Richard," she said as she stood and took him by the hand, "stay the night with me until you sleep and recover. I will sit on this chair while you sleep on the couch, and in the morning, I will prepare breakfast. Then you can be on your way."

CHAPTER TWENTY

ACCEPTANCE

Richard let the phone ring. He didn't want to take the chance that Anita was calling. He was not yet ready to speak with her. He thought it was reasonable Cassandra would have informed Anita of his experience in her tent during the course of their normal interaction. He needed more time to think before he interacted with others. The experience in the tent had been vivid and exhilarating if not somewhat exhausting. What was the relevance to the origin of religion? He sat in the recliner and took a sip of hot coffee. He had been drinking the dark brew frequently in an effort to return to his normal sober state. He began to analyze his experience in Cassandra's tent.

Cassandra had told him that he had been in the tent for six hours. He could only remember entering the tent with her, watching her light the fire and leaving. He remembered sitting to relax, and at that point in his experience, his thoughts seemed to merge into a brief dreamlike memory. He realized that what his dreamlike experience entailed was likely memories that he had read or experienced. His recall of the scene he witnessed of the three priests in front of the altar paying homage to the aligned planets in the heavens remained vivid in his mind. It bore a striking resemblance to a photograph that appeared in a printed newspaper article about the Conference of Catholic Bishops he had read. The photograph showed a priest speaking to an audience. Behind the priest was a large painting of God, the Father, and Jesus and in front of both, the Virgin Mary. All were surrounded by halos. The alignment and depiction of the figures bore a striking resemblance to the planets Saturn, Venus, and Mars that he had observed in his dreamlike trance.

Was his dream of standing with the multitude at the base of Mount Sinai simply a memory of what he had read and heard about as a youngster reading the Bible? It was likely that the effect of the drug released memories without the semblance of time, and it appeared to him to be in present time. If that was the case, then it was likely that in some recorded incidences, the ancients were not communicating with God so much as hallucinating in a dreamlike trance with memories from not only their personal unconscious but also with the collective unconscious and perhaps with memories of legends and myth. The effect would have been to convince them that they were in communication with the divine, especially if they participated in a mass experience over an extended period.

A terrifying thought occurred to him. Had he journeyed into the collective unconscious? If so, this vicarious journey back into time, into the collective memory of the human race, could have been a hideous and horrid experience. Had he been fortunate to have experienced relatively benign images during his experience? He shuddered at the possible dark archetypes that might lie in the collective unconscious.

He was convinced that this one experience was not enough to make a judgment of the effect of the psychoactive drugs on the ancients' religion. He decided he would not personally experience its effects again but would further study the literature to seek insight into its significance, if any. He was certain that the rabbis would have commented on its use either in the Mishnah or Talmud. He would search the literature to determine if the use of psychoactive drugs played a prominent part in the commentaries.

Richard took another sip of coffee, inhaled deeply, held his breath for several seconds, and then slowly exhaled through pursed lips in an attempt to relax and think of something else.

Michael and Shura had completed their debriefings with the Border Patrol and had flown to Mexico City to spend time with Shura's family. Before they had left, Michael had confided in him that the experience with the Border Patrol had made him realize how close he had come to losing his bride. Her father had offered him a position in the family business with a good salary. Shura appeared to be making a steady recovery, and he wanted to be with her during her convalescence. They had put their plans for further education temporarily aside but not the plans for starting a family. He had told Richard that they were probably committed to Mexico City for at least a year, if not permanently. He assured his father that they would visit as often as possible. There were direct flights from Mexico City to Phoenix, so it would not be a lengthy flight. Although Richard was sad to see them leave, he knew it was good for them. He also resolved to further concentrate on his work and complete it.

There was something about his experience in the tent that seemed familiar, but he was having difficulty remembering what it was. Was it similar to meditation? Richard had expanded the relaxation and self-hypnosis techniques he had learned in the navy to basic meditation, which had helped him. He remembered that on one of his dinner dates with Jane Barker, they had attended a lecture at the Unity Church in the foothills given by a woman who was an experienced neuroscientist. In her lecture, she had described how she had changed her perception of human awareness or consciousness from simply a neural function of the brain into something greater in which the brain served as a facilitator of consciousness but that consciousness was not solely produced by the brain. He recalled her presentation in which she presented a cogent argument that there was a universal consciousness and that humans were able to access it and even communicate with it through various experiences, including meditation.

Is this work becoming too complex? he wondered? *The electric universe paradigm was an interdisciplinary one, and neuroscience and meditation were disciplines that were relevant. It didn't matter what type of physical events took place in ancient times if there were no humans to witness them. He was seeking to find the origin of religion, but the origin was not in the physical events themselves but in the human perception of them. It was from these first perceptions that humans developed the complex theologies and rituals that exist today, theologies so complex and influenced by belief that they obscured the origins he sought. Perhaps this was the insight he had gained in the tent in which he burned incense to the Queen of Heaven.*

Richard reached to the telephone base unit and pressed the replay button on the recorder.

"Hello, Richard. This is Anita. I've been wondering about you since I haven't heard from you in a couple of days. I spoke with Cassandra, and although she was somewhat reluctant to tell what happened when you visited her, I was able to convince her to do so. She told me that you spent about six hours in her tent with her slowly burning marijuana mixture or what she insists on calling incense similar to that used by the Israelites. She said that you had experienced the effects of the drug and had exited the tent somewhat confused and disoriented. At least she was thoughtful enough to have you sleep on the couch until you recovered enough to drive home safely. Why haven't you called me? I am worried about you and want to get together with you as soon as I can. If I don't receive a call from you, I'll drive over to your place to check on you."

Richard decided not to call her because he was positive she would arrive shortly. He knew her to be a determined woman and would not hesitate to do what she said. He quickly tidied up the house and showered and shaved. He hadn't done either since he had left Cassandra's house. He heard a car pull up into the drive just as he was buttoning his shirt. He quickly slipped on his slippers and went to the door to greet her.

"Hi, Anita. I'm so glad you came. I didn't realize until today that I'm still not quite over my experience in Cassandra's tent. Let me help you with the bags. What's in them?"

"Hello, Richard. It's good to see you relatively well. I've brought some homemade albondigas soup, rice, and tortillas. Have you eaten yet?"

"No, and I just realized I'm hungry. Come into the kitchen, and I'll warm up the soup and tortillas. What kind of rice is it?"

"It's yellow Mexican rice. Many people put rice in it, but some prefer not to do so. I'll let you try it without and with the rice. You sit down, Richard. I'll do the cooking. Do you want something to drink?"

"No, thanks. I've had three cups of coffee. I appreciate you doing this for me, Anita."

She looked at him and smiled. She bent over him and kissed him.

"I don't know what you experienced in the tent, Richard. Cassandra is convinced that you experienced something similar to what the ancients did in their relationships with the Lord. Try a spoonful of rice in the soup to see how you like it."

He did as she said and tasted the soup. It was delicious, and its warmth spread through his body like a comforting blanket of contentment. He remembered his mother used to make albondigas soup. Memories of him as a youth sitting in the kitchen with his father, sister, and mother seemed like only yesterday. The memory also brought an awareness of his life as one continuous thread woven into a greater, all-encompassing fabric of life and its purpose. He recalled speaking with friends in the entrance lobby of the Unity Church that night after the lecture he had attended with Jane Barker. There were several pieces of literature on the table where books and other media were available. He had picked a small card the size of a bookmark and had read several items on it that were titled "Five Basic Unity

Principles." He couldn't remember all of them but two whose words struck him with their insight:

There is only one Presence and one Power active as the Universe, God the Good;

Our essence is God: therefore, we are inherently good. This God essence called the Christ was fully expressed as Jesus.[29]

There were others he couldn't remember. Jesus was a Jew like him, and his first disciples were all Jews, including, he believed, Mary Magdalene. Jesus Himself said He had come to teach man that the kingdom of heaven was within us. The name of the woman who gave the lecture had rigorously studied the experiences of patients who had experienced a near-death experience, NDE. She had related how she had learned meditation and had done so for decades. She had experienced some of the emotions or effects from her meditation that were not unlike some of those who had experienced NDE. For the first time, Richard realized he was beginning to understand. It seems the catastrophic occurrences that humankind experienced could be deeply embedded into the human psyche and emerge from the collective unconscious into an individual's conscious awareness, a conscious awareness that could attain communion with a greater consciousness prevalent in the universe. Perhaps this is the presence in the universe that is God.

He looked across the table at Anita sitting and looking at him with deep interest. She was beautiful with her black hair, brown eyes, and olive skin. She smiled as if to ask what he was thinking. He smiled back but didn't speak.

"Richard," she said, "I realize that you've had some type of spiritual experience under the influence of Cassandra's incense. I know you well enough by now that you are earnestly seeking

---

[29] Unity.org (Unity of Tucson, 2016).

an understanding of what your life is all about and you are seeking this through your work on the origin of religion. You've mentioned that your hope is that somehow your work will help others perceive the origin of religion. You're convinced that the origin was based on natural events that humankind could not understand the causes of and these events served as the foundation for religion, astronomy, and astrology. You mentioned that perhaps this will help us start to understand how mankind can learn from this knowledge and, in some way, make progress toward a better world. I admire your optimism, but I remain skeptical. But my burning question to you is, how will this affect your personally? What do you hope to gain from this?"

Richard was struck, speechless by her question. In the back of his mind, he had thought perhaps he would receive a clearer understanding of life and of the universe. He had thought perhaps that a revelation would come to him like the violent awakening of the ancient prophets in the scriptures. He knew that it was not to be. He sensed a brief passing realization that he could remain alone in an uncaring universe without a foundation to lean on if he abandoned the foundation on which his life had been built.

He looked at the questioning eyes of the beautiful woman who sat across the table from him. He would face whatever future lay before him with or without a better understanding than when he began his project, but he wanted desperately to share that future with her.

Anita smiled as she looked at him fondly.

"Richard, did you just ask me to marry you?" she asked.

"Yes," he replied.

185

Printed in the United States
By Bookmasters